POSSESSIONS™

BOOK FOUR

THE FINAL TANTRUM

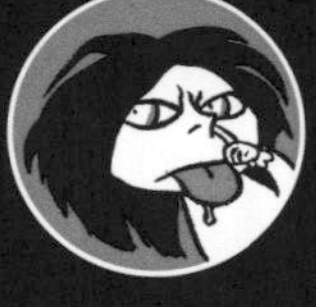

GURGAZON
THE UNCLEAN

Nasty and snide

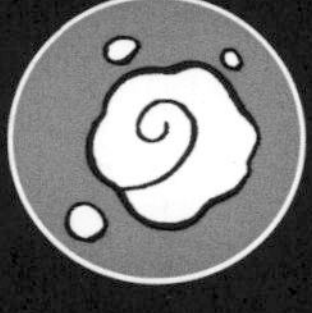

THE ICE FIELD
LIGHTS

So cold he died

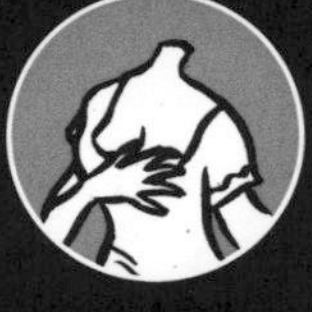

THE PALE
LADY

Victim of pride

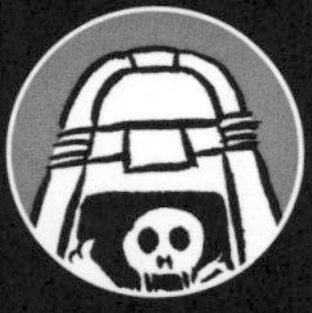

THE
DUKE

Haunted and fried

THE STURMANN
POLTERGEIST
AKA "POLLY"

Nature defied

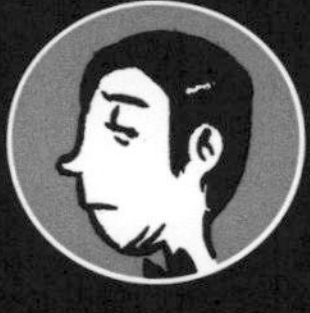

MR.
THORNE

Extremely keen-eyed

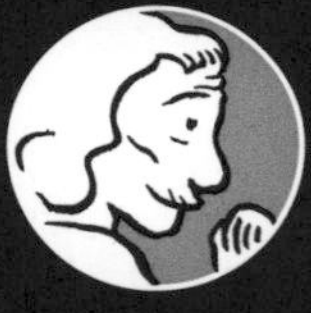

MS.
LLEWELLYN-VANE

Most satisfied

POSSESSIONS

BOOK FOUR
THE FINAL TANTRUM

WRITTEN & ILLUSTRATED BY
RAY FAWKES

DESIGN BY
KEITH WOOD

EDITED BY
JILL BEATON & ROBIN HERRERA

Oni Press, Inc.

PUBLISHER **Joe Nozemack** · EDITOR IN CHIEF **James Lucas Jones**

V.P. OF BUSINESS DEVELOPMENT **Tim Wiesch**

DIRECTOR OF SALES **Cheyenne Allott** · DIRECTOR OF PUBLICITY **John Schork**

PRODUCTION MANAGER **Troy Look** · SENIOR DESIGNER **Jason Storey**

EDITOR **Charlie Chu** · ASSOCIATE EDITOR **Robin Herrera**

INVENTORY COORDINATOR **Brad Rooks**

ADMINISTRATIVE ASSISTANT **Ari Yarwood** · OFFICE ASSISTANT **Jung Lee**

PRODUCTION ASSISTANT **Jared Jones**

Possessions, Volume 4, February 2015. Published by Oni Press, Inc.
1305 SE Martin Luther King Jr. Blvd., Suite A, Portland, OR 97214.
Possessions is ™ & © 2015 Ray Fawkes and Piper Snow Productions, Ltd.

Oni Press Inc.
1305 SE Martin Luther King Jr. Blvd.
Suite A
Portland, OR 97214

onipress.com · facebook.com/onipress
twitter.com/onipress · onipress.tumblr.com

First Edition: February 2015

ISBN: 978-1-62010-015-8 • eISBN: 978-1-62010-053-0

Library of Congress Control Number: 2014944755

1 3 5 7 9 10 8 6 4 2

PRINTED IN CHINA

THIS ONE'S FOR **BEANS.**

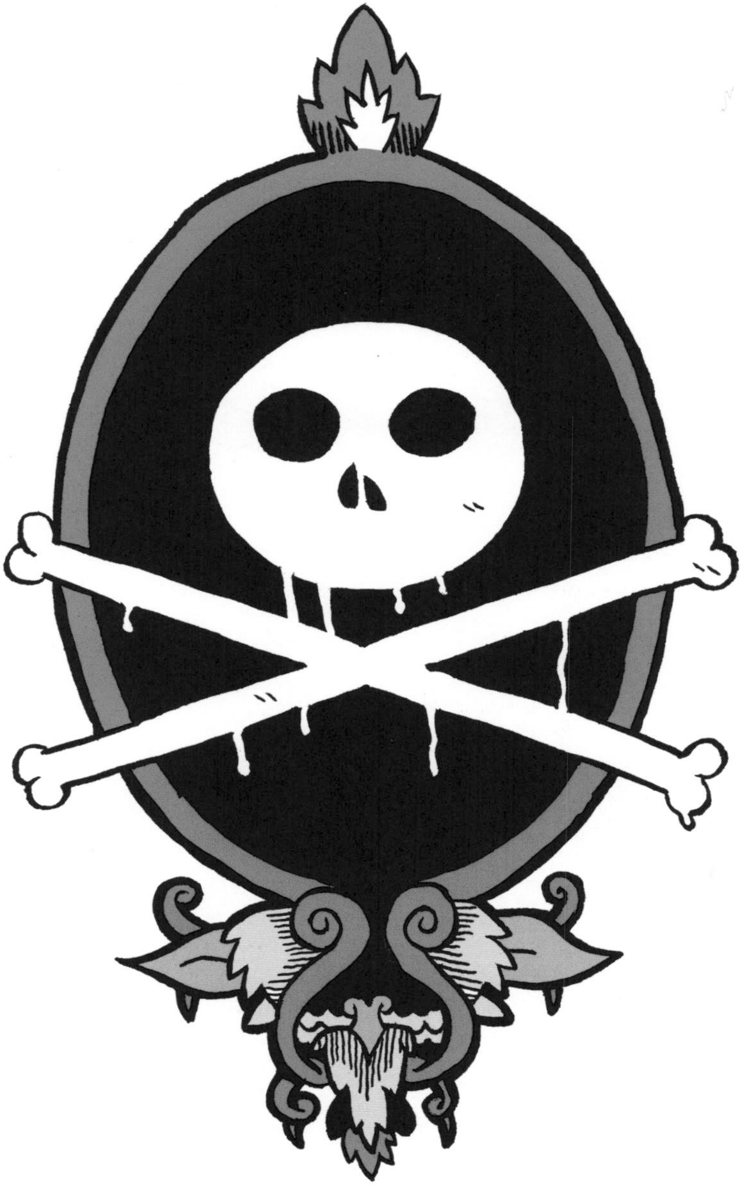

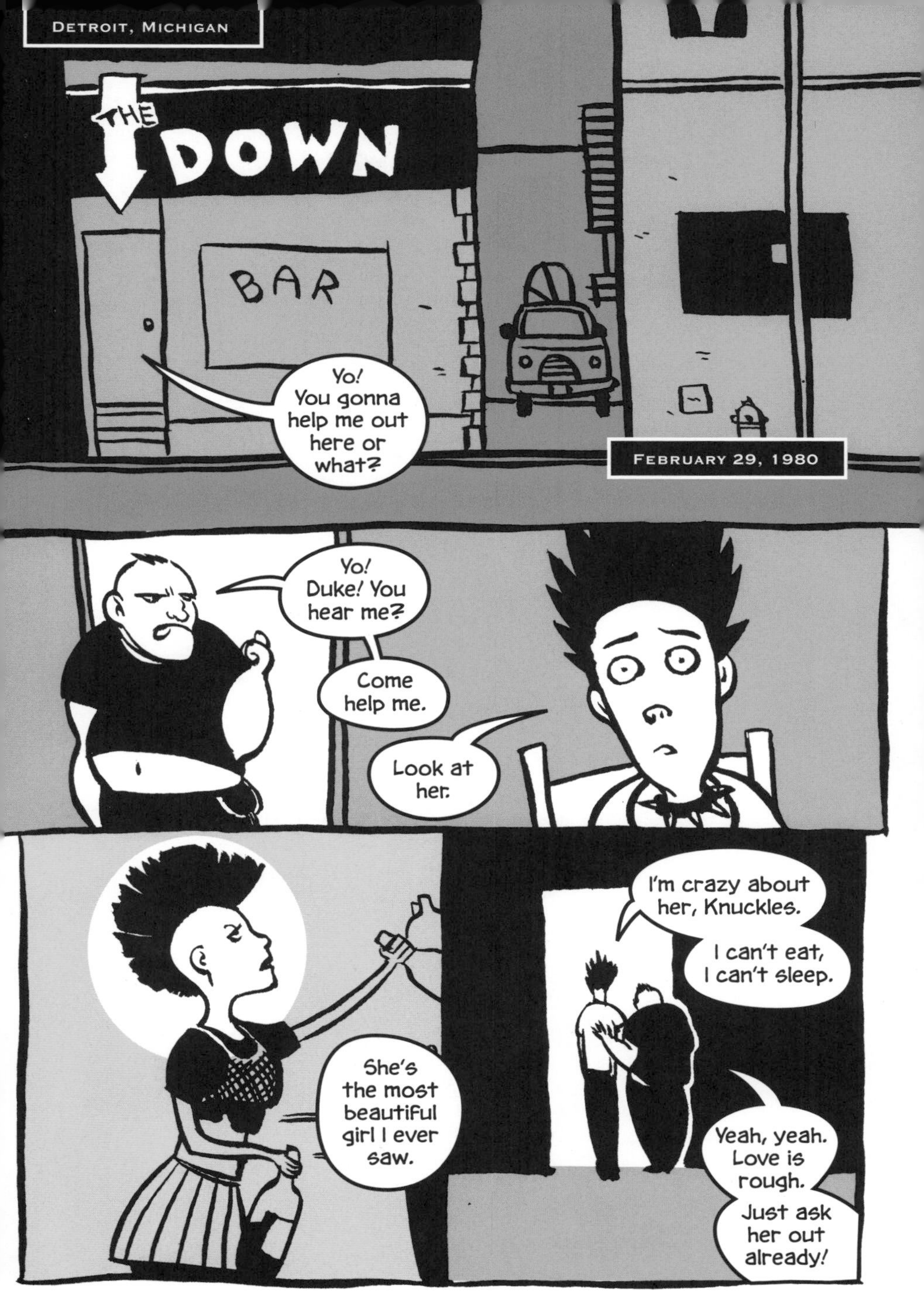
Detroit, Michigan
THE DOWN
BAR
Yo! You gonna help me out here or what?
February 29, 1980
Yo! Duke! You hear me?
Come help me.
Look at her.
I'm crazy about her, Knuckles.
I can't eat, I can't sleep.
She's the most beautiful girl I ever saw.
Yeah, yeah. Love is rough.
Just ask her out already!

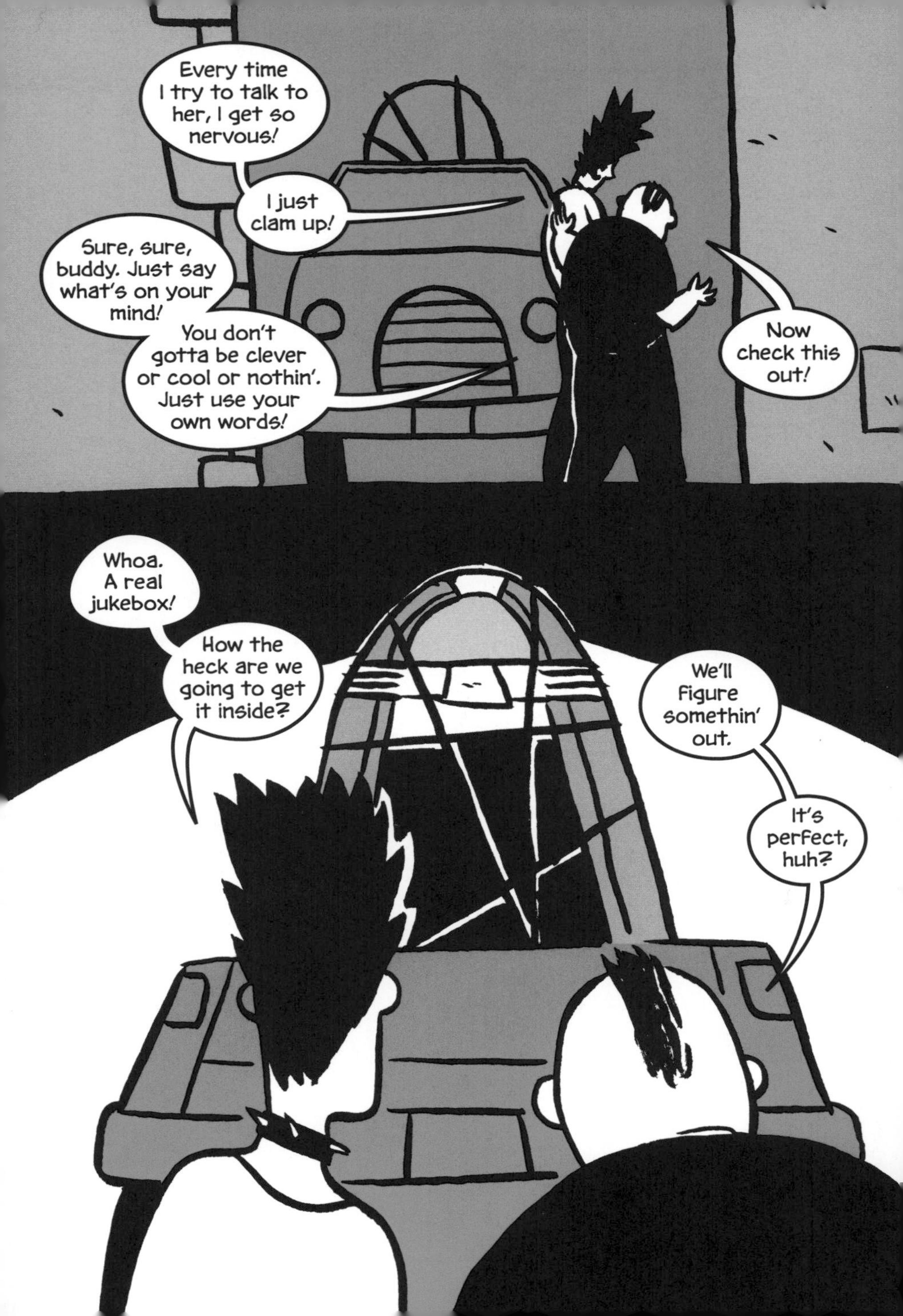
Every time I try to talk to her, I get so nervous!
I just clam up!
Sure, sure, buddy. Just say what's on your mind!
You don't gotta be clever or cool or nothin'. Just use your own words!
Now check this out!
Whoa. A real jukebox!
How the heck are we going to get it inside?
We'll figure somethin' out.
It's perfect, huh?

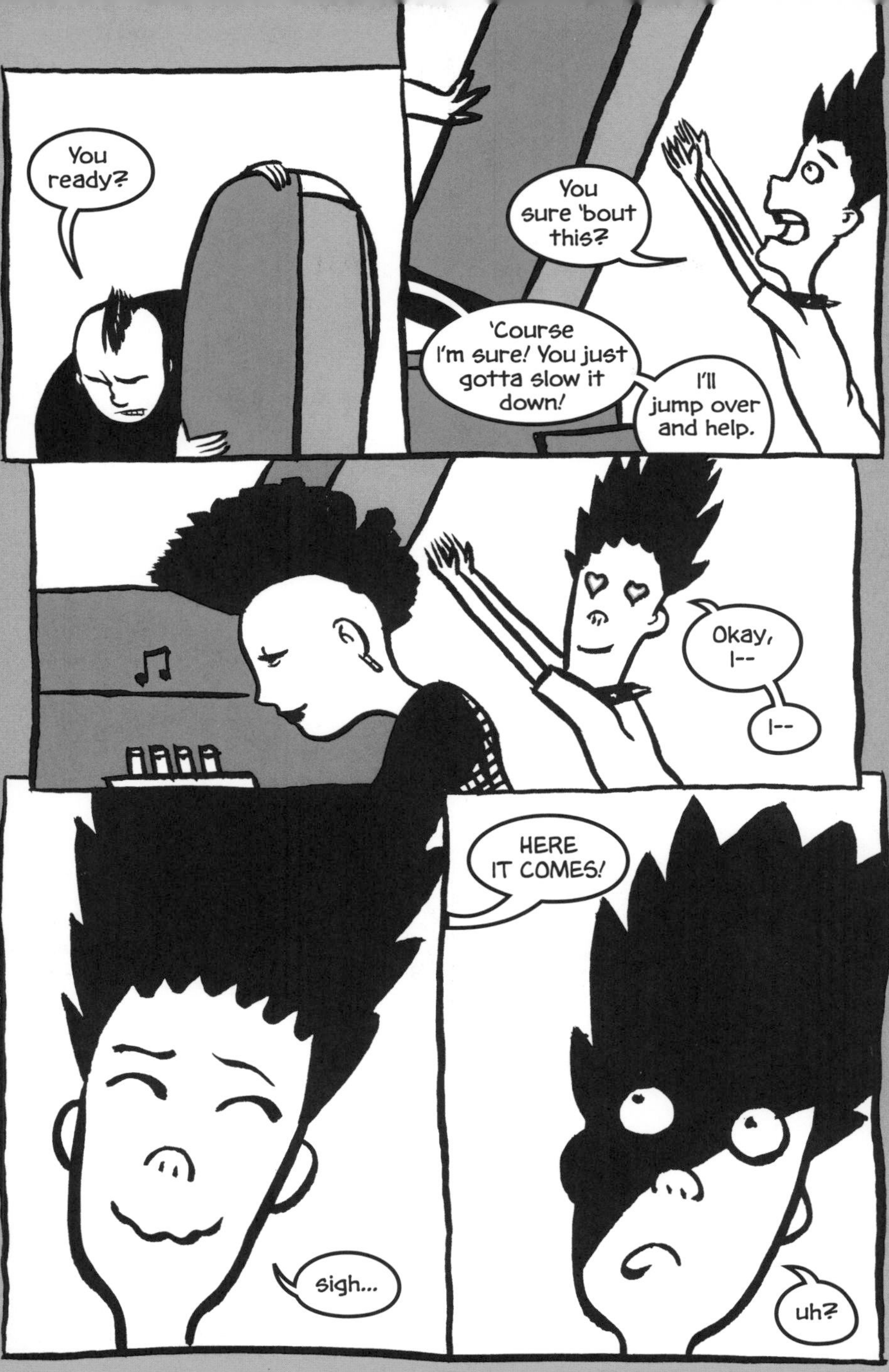
You ready?
You sure 'bout this?
'Course I'm sure! You just gotta slow it down!
I'll jump over and help.
Okay, I--
I--
HERE IT COMES!
sigh...
uh?

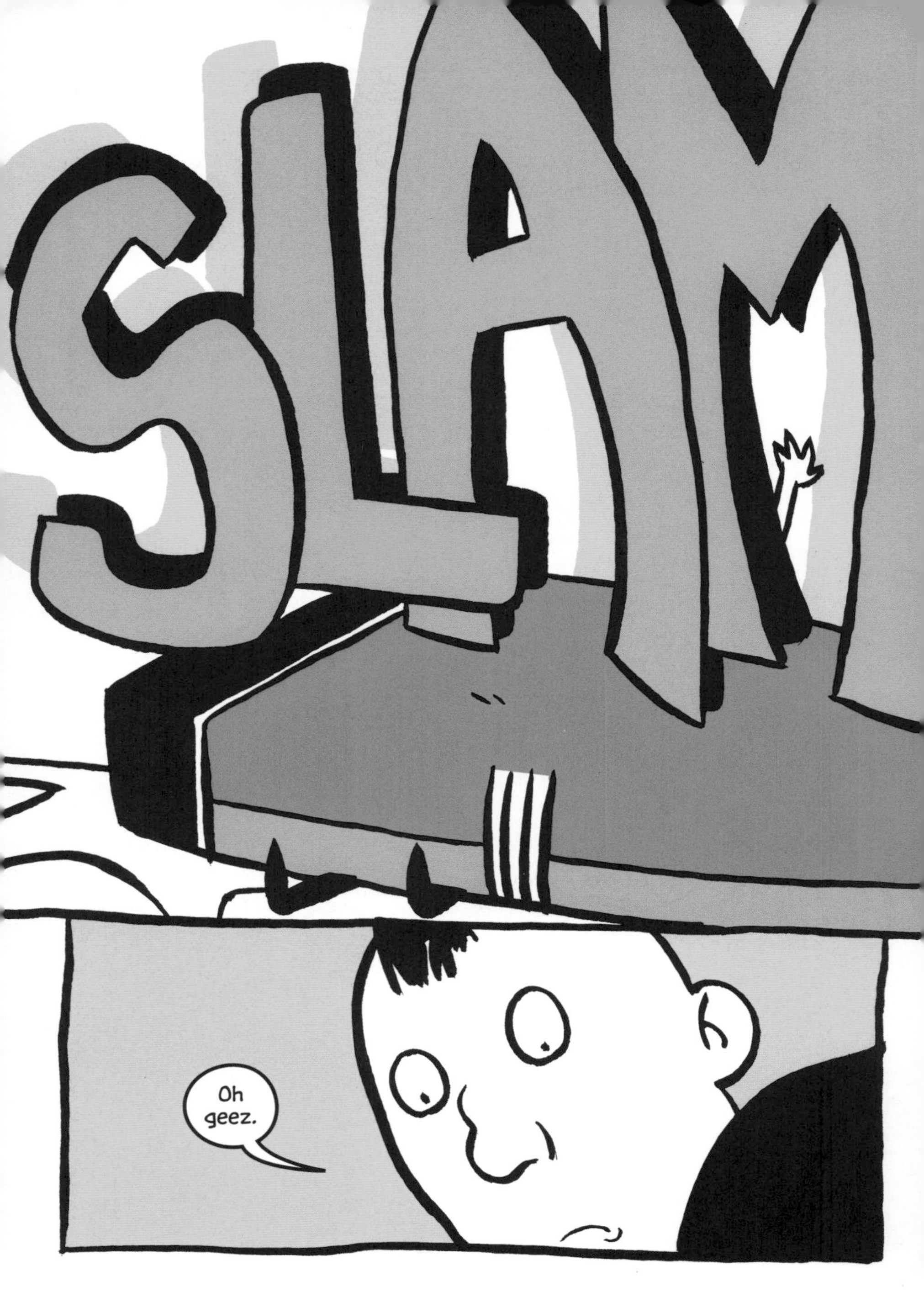
SLAM
Oh geez.

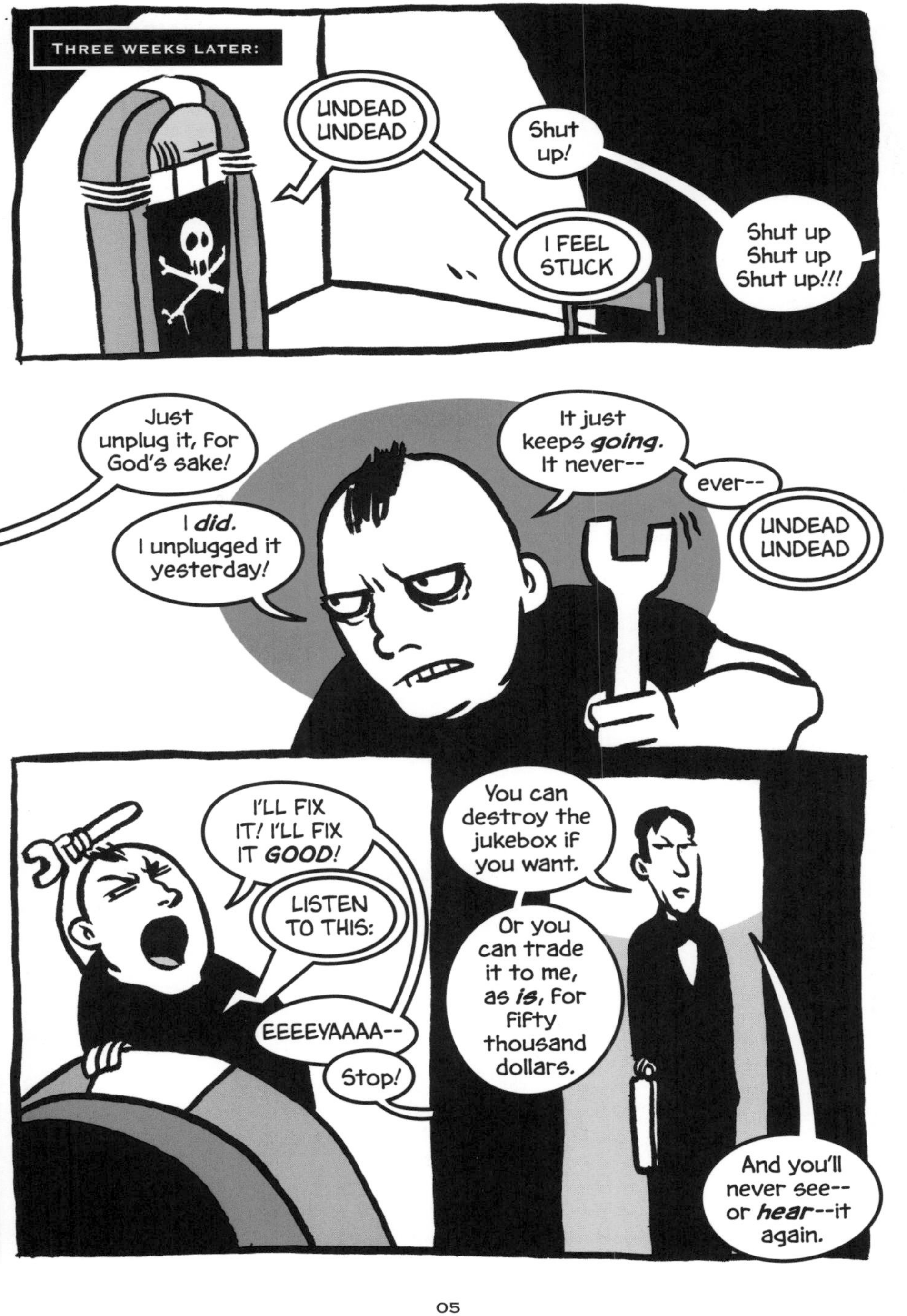
THREE WEEKS LATER:
UNDEAD UNDEAD
Shut up!
I FEEL STUCK
Shut up Shut up Shut up!!!
Just unplug it, for God's sake!
I *did.* I unplugged it yesterday!
It just keeps *going.* It never--
ever--
UNDEAD UNDEAD
I'LL FIX IT! I'LL FIX IT *GOOD!*
LISTEN TO THIS:
EEEEYAAAA--
Stop!
You can destroy the jukebox if you want.
Or you can trade it to me, as *is,* for fifty thousand dollars.
And you'll never see-- or *hear*--it again.

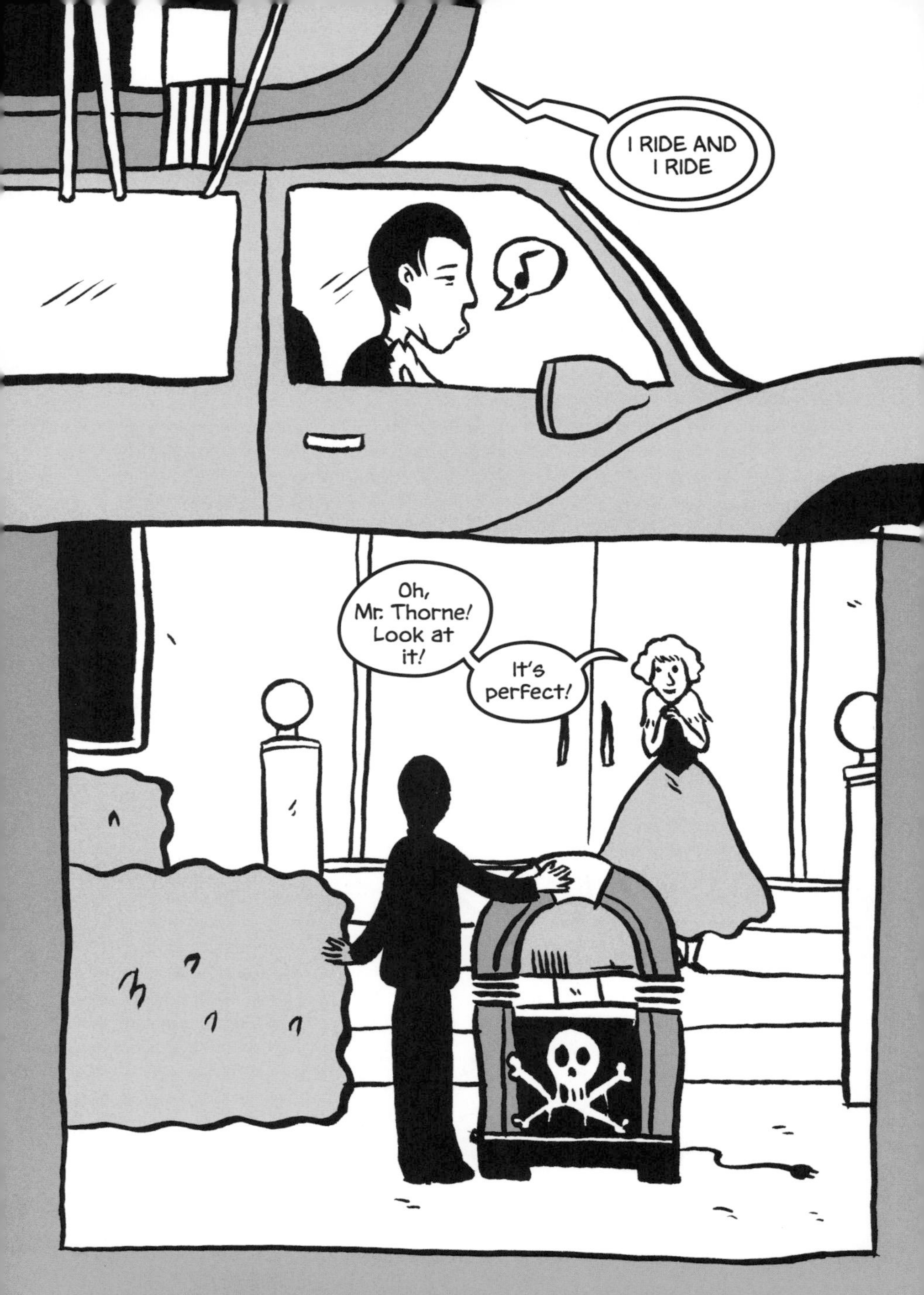
I RIDE AND I RIDE
Oh, Mr. Thorne! Look at it!
It's perfect!

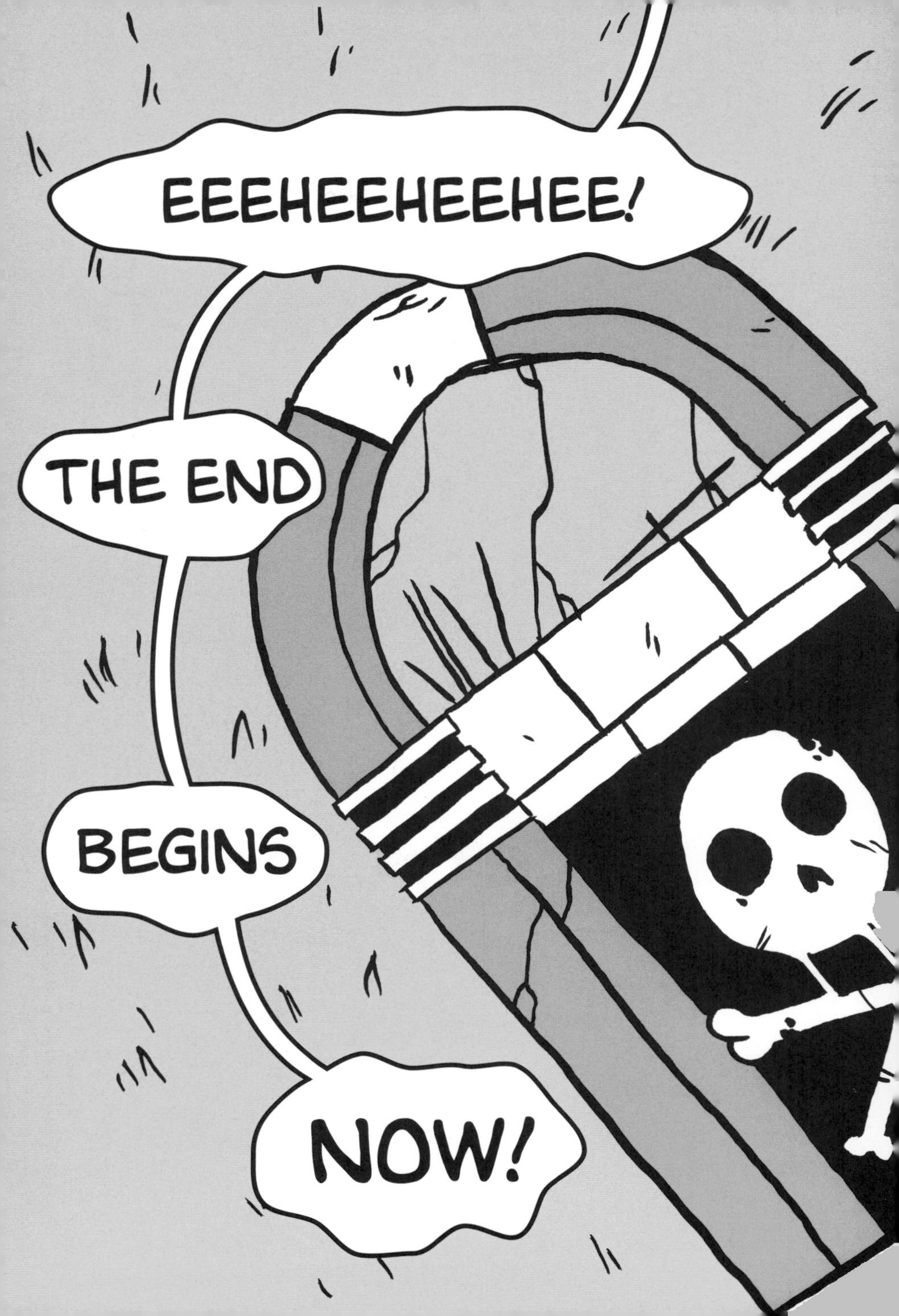
EEEHEEHEEHEE!
THE END
BEGINS
NOW!

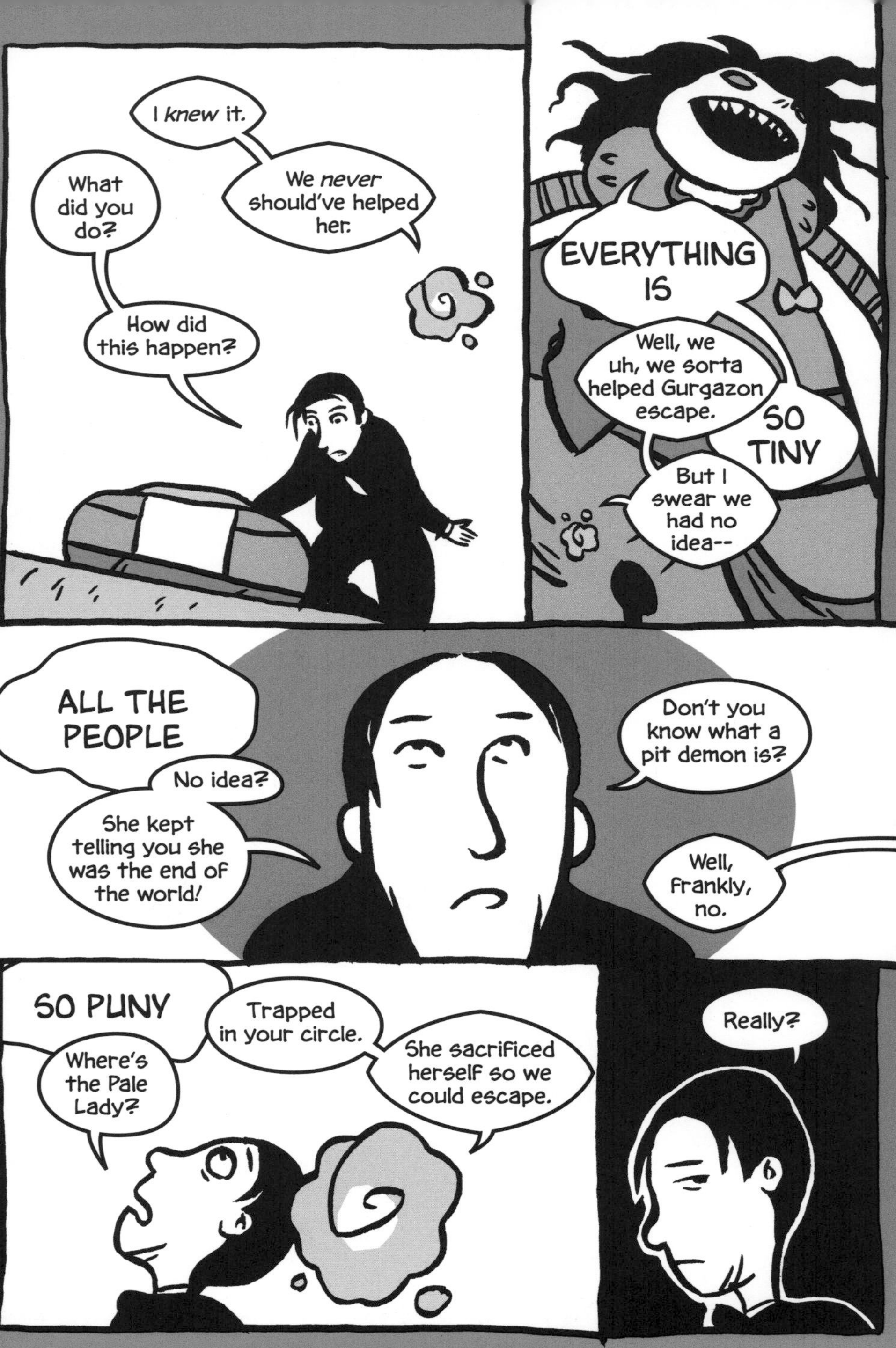

I *knew* it.
We *never* should've helped her.
What did you do?
How did this happen?
EVERYTHING IS
Well, we uh, we sorta helped Gurgazon escape.
SO TINY
But I swear we had no idea--
ALL THE PEOPLE
No idea?
She kept telling you she was the end of the world!
Don't you know what a pit demon is?
Well, frankly, no.
SO PUNY
Trapped in your circle.
Where's the Pale Lady?
She sacrificed herself so we could escape.
Really?

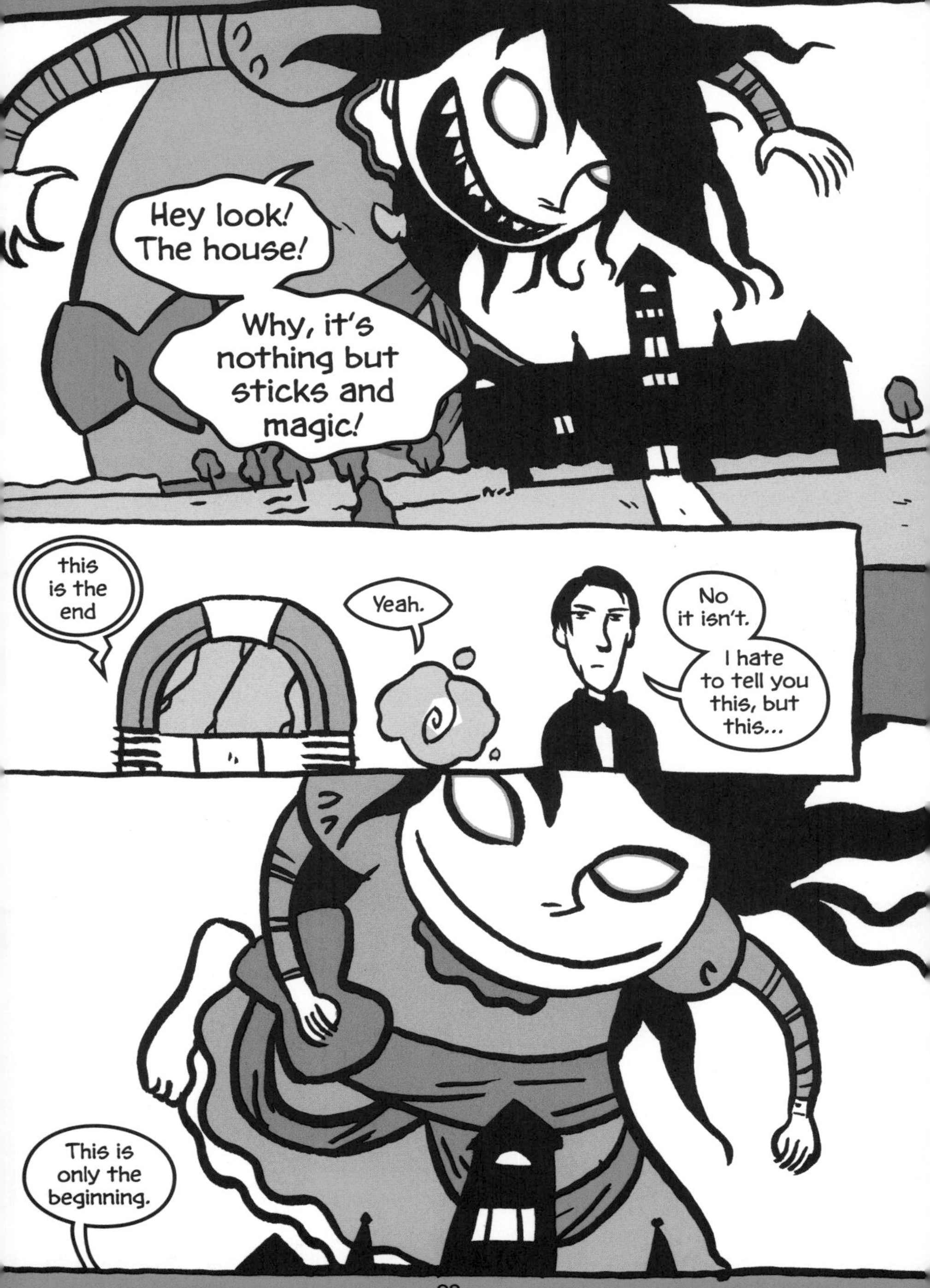
Hey look! The house!
Why, it's nothing but sticks and magic!
this is the end
Yeah.
No it isn't.
I hate to tell you this, but this...
This is only the beginning.

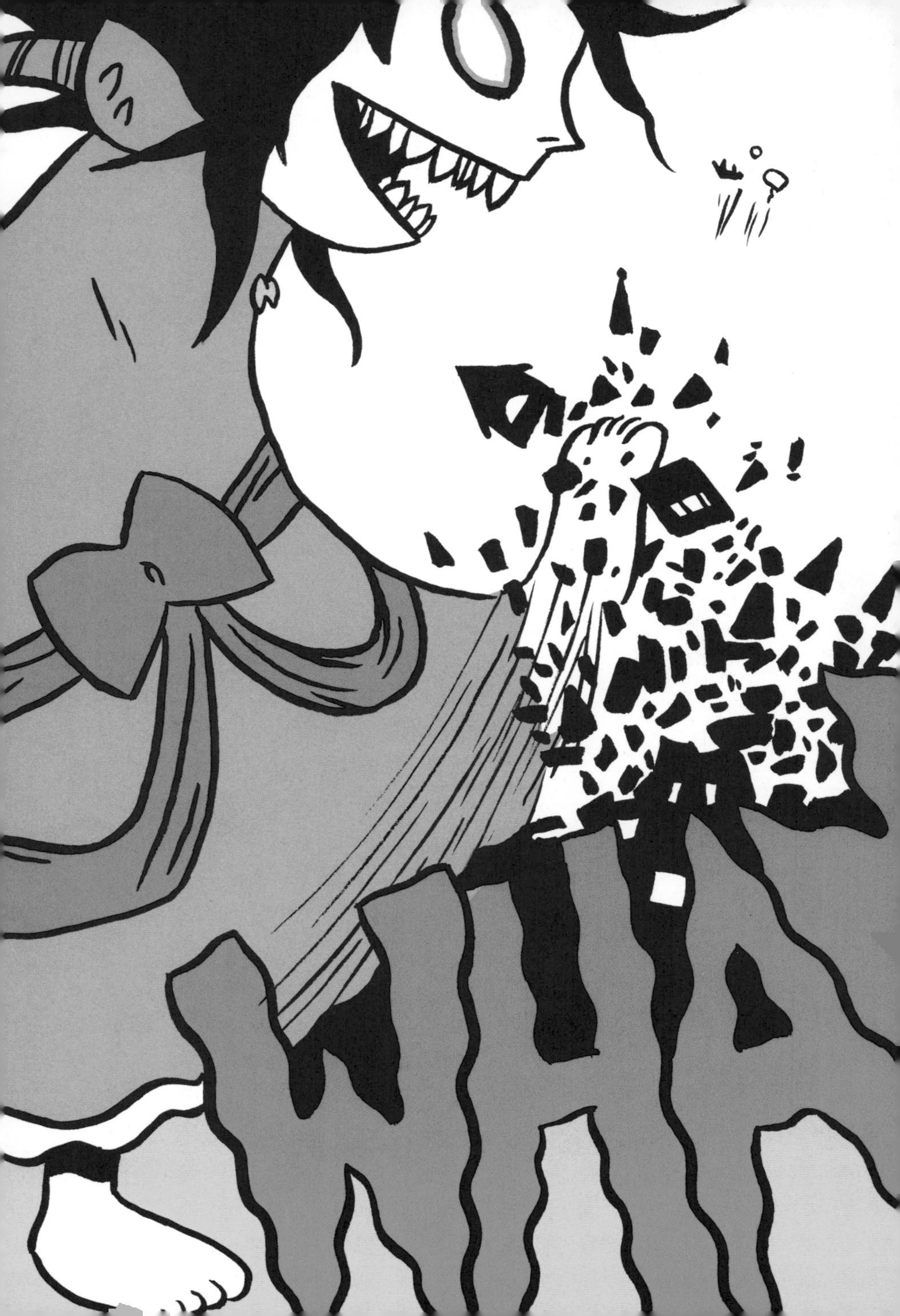

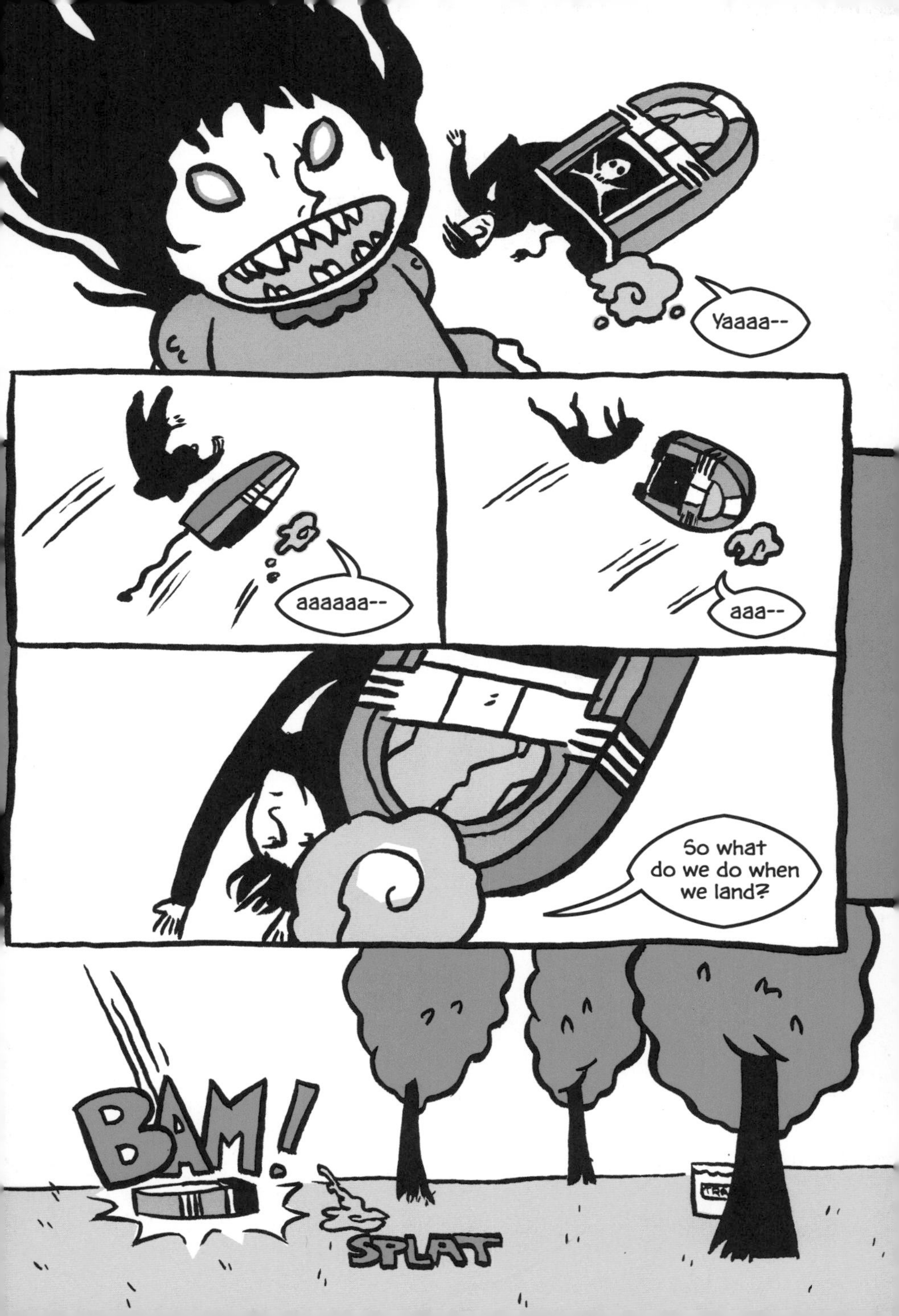
Yaaaa--
aaaaaa--
aaa--
So what do we do when we land?
BAM!
SPLAT

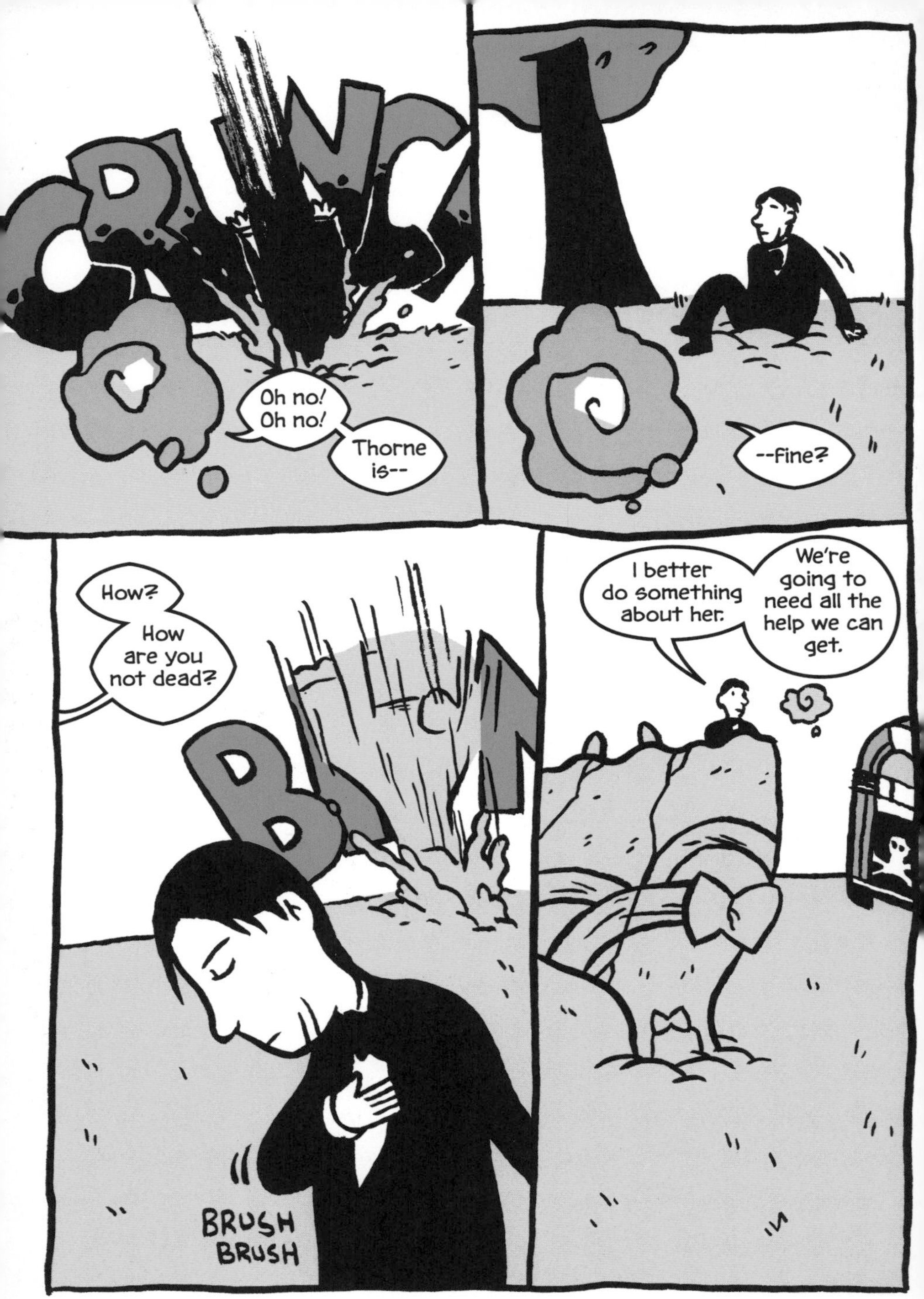
Oh no!
Oh no!
Thorne is--
--fine?
How?
How are you not dead?
BRUSH BRUSH
I better do something about her.
We're going to need all the help we can get.

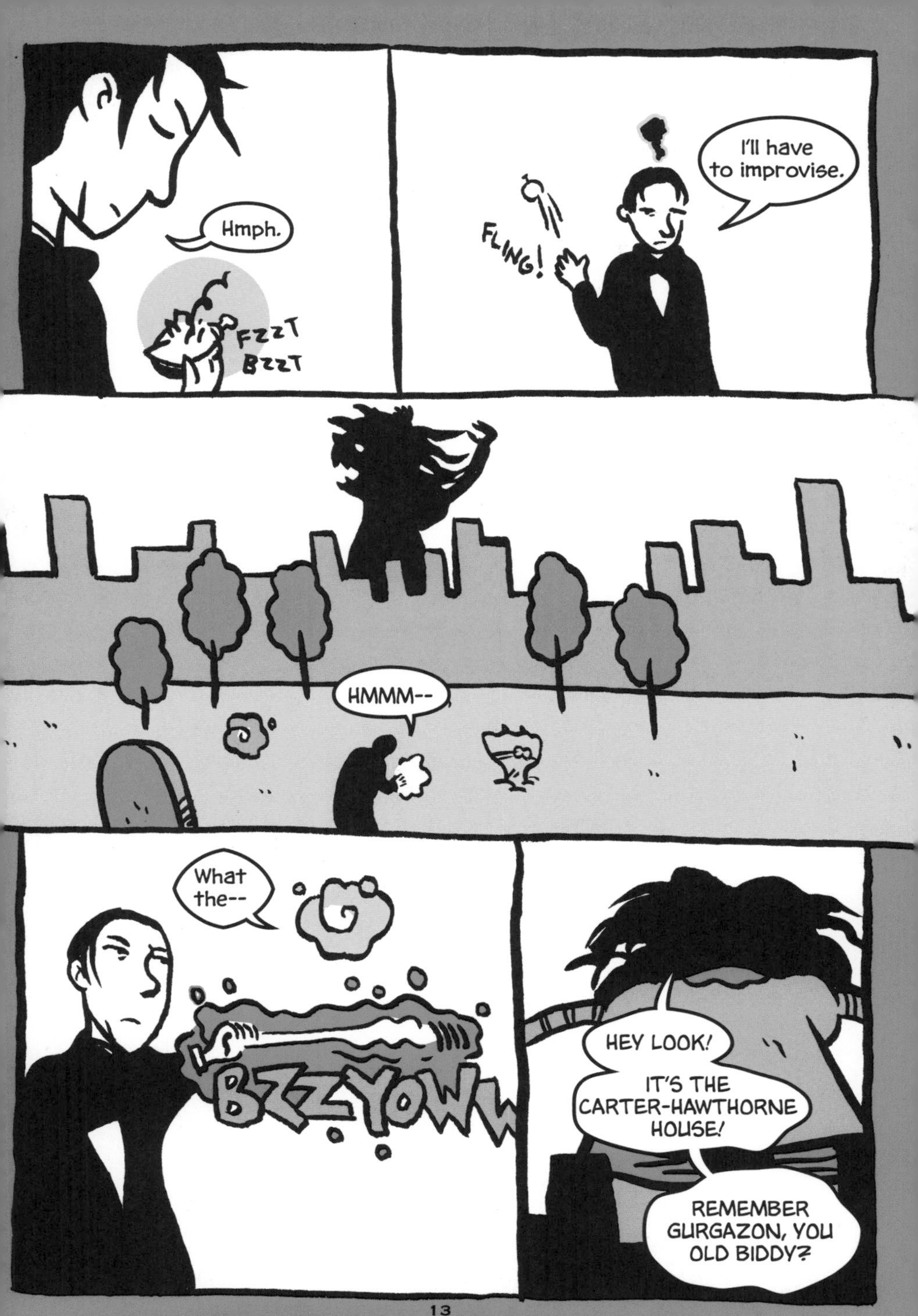
Hmph.
FZZT
BZZT
FLING!
I'll have to improvise.
HMMM--
What the--
BZZYOWW
HEY LOOK!
IT'S THE CARTER-HAWTHORNE HOUSE!
REMEMBER GURGAZON, YOU OLD BIDDY?

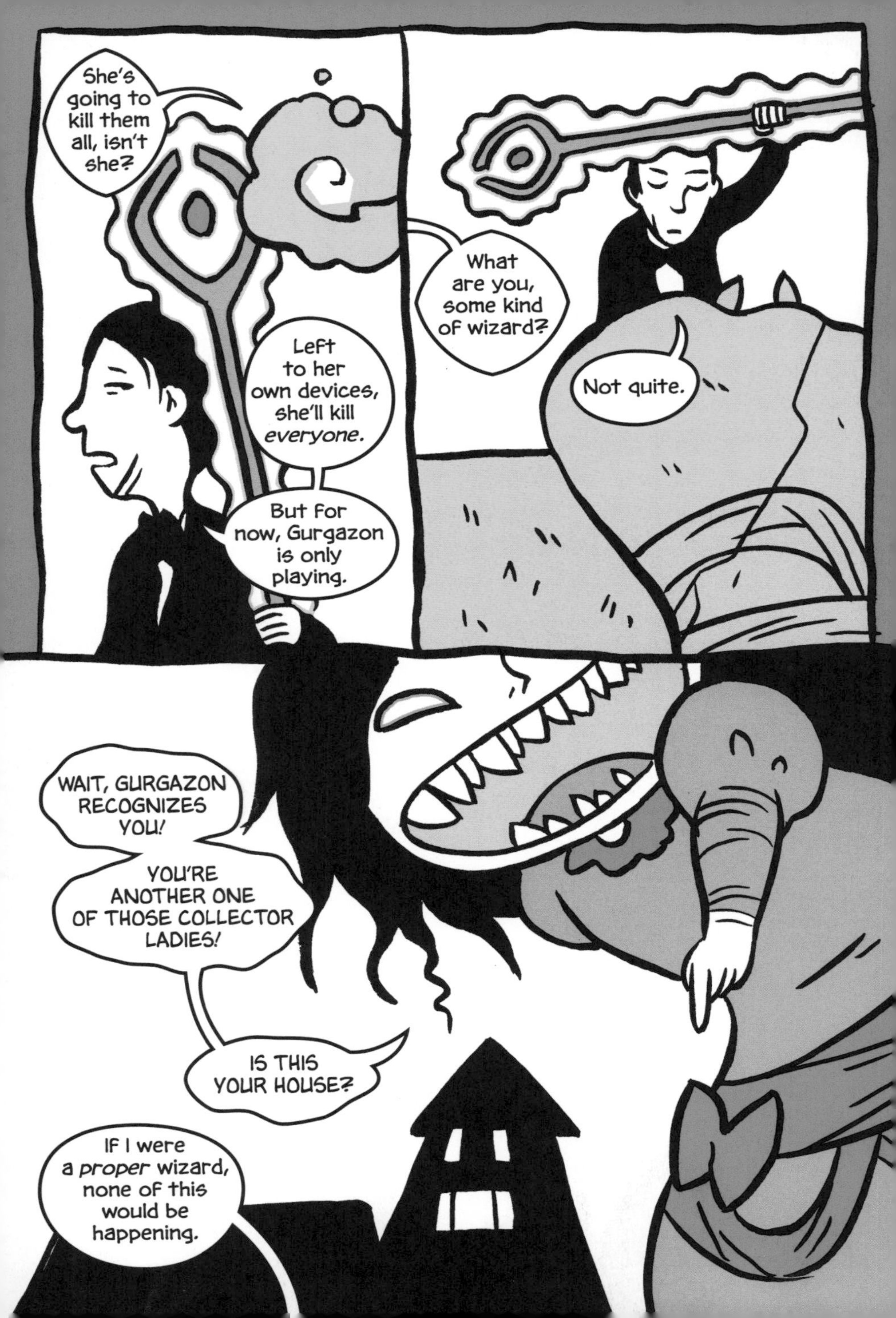
She's going to kill them all, isn't she?
Left to her own devices, she'll kill *everyone*.
But for now, Gurgazon is only playing.
What are you, some kind of wizard?
Not quite.
WAIT, GURGAZON RECOGNIZES YOU!
YOU'RE ANOTHER ONE OF THOSE COLLECTOR LADIES!
IS THIS YOUR HOUSE?
If I were a *proper* wizard, none of this would be happening.

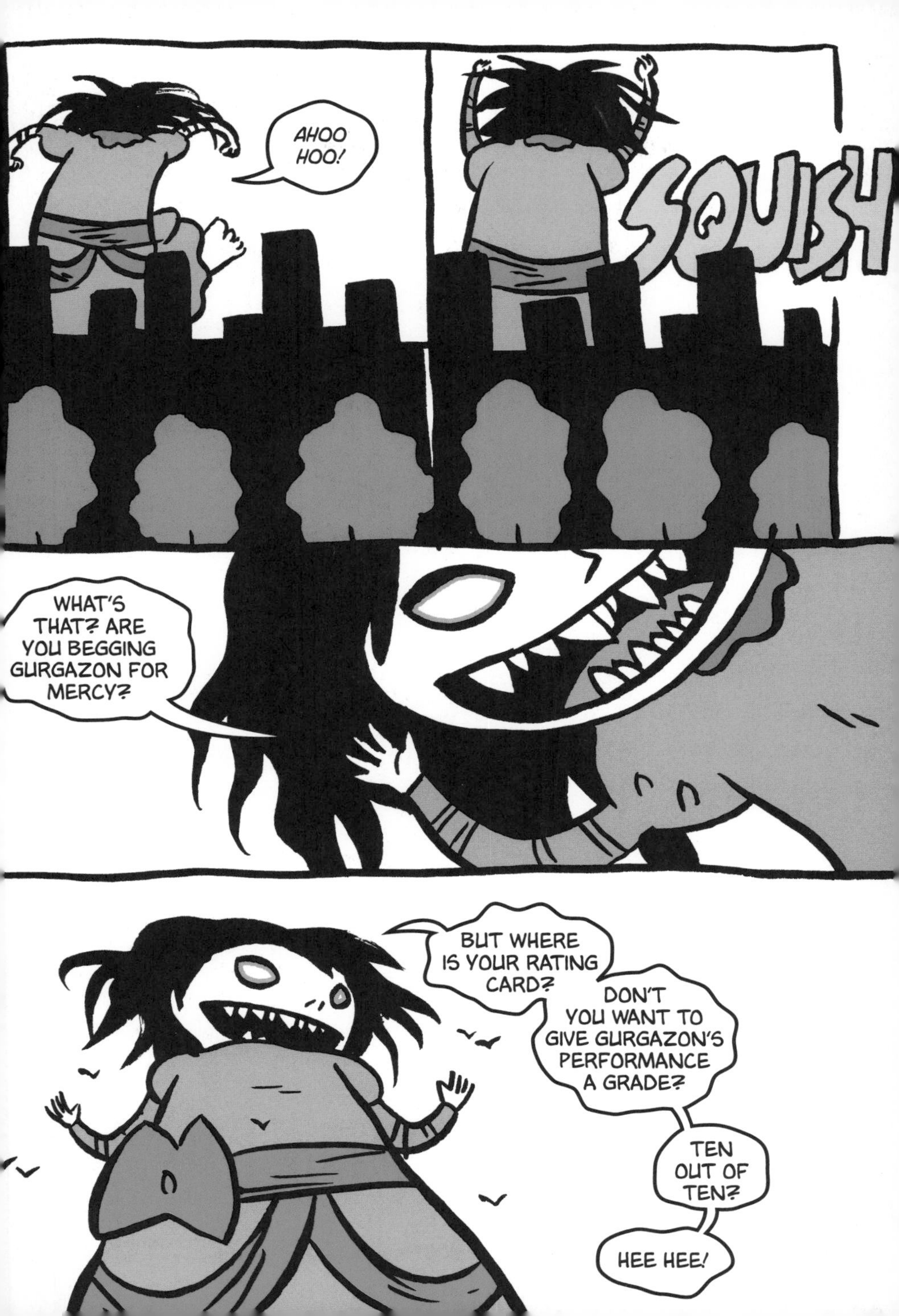
AHOO HOO!
SQUISH
WHAT'S THAT? ARE YOU BEGGING GURGAZON FOR MERCY?
BUT WHERE IS YOUR RATING CARD?
DON'T YOU WANT TO GIVE GURGAZON'S PERFORMANCE A GRADE?
TEN OUT OF TEN?
HEE HEE!

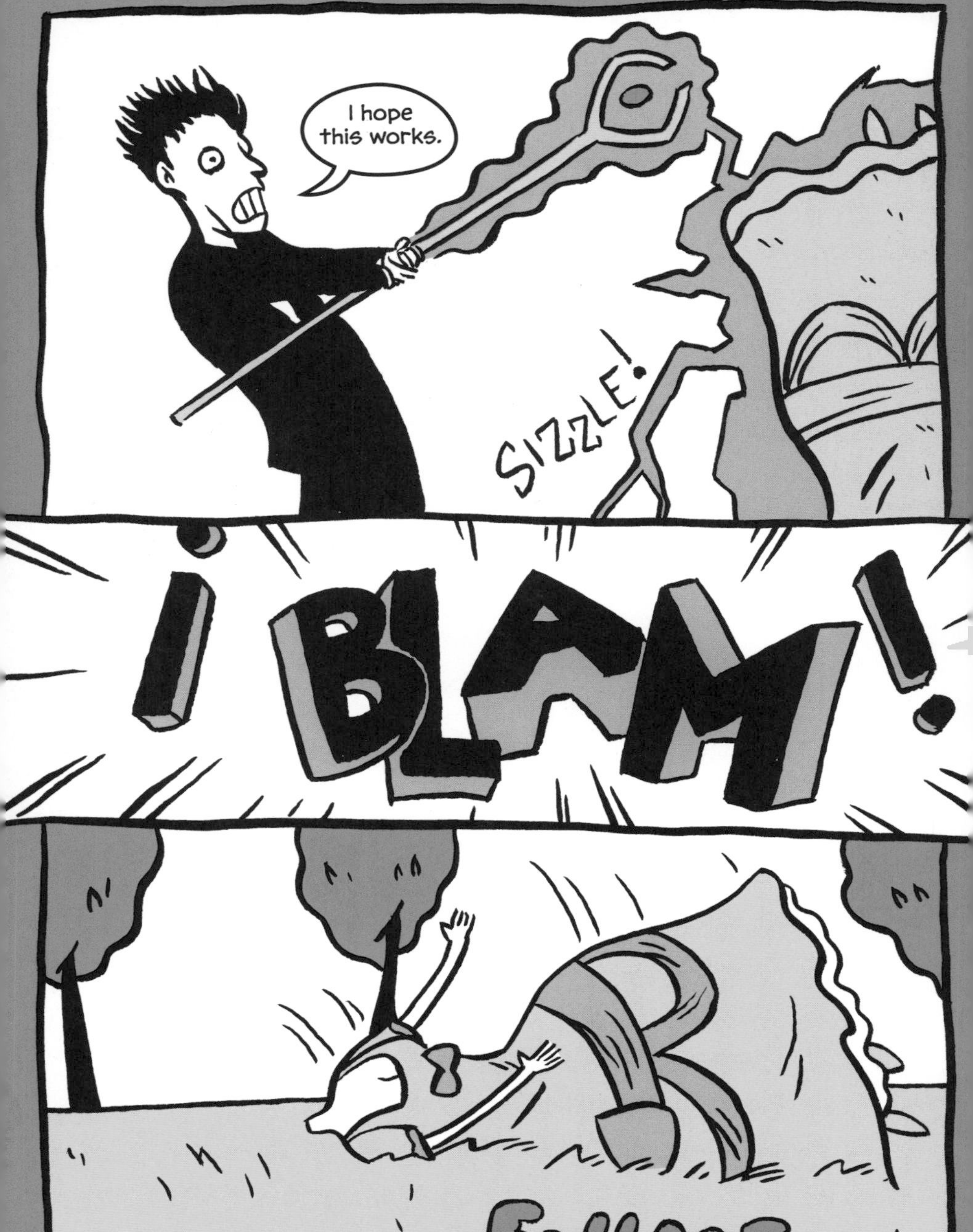
I hope this works.
SIZZLE!
¡BLAM!
FLUMF

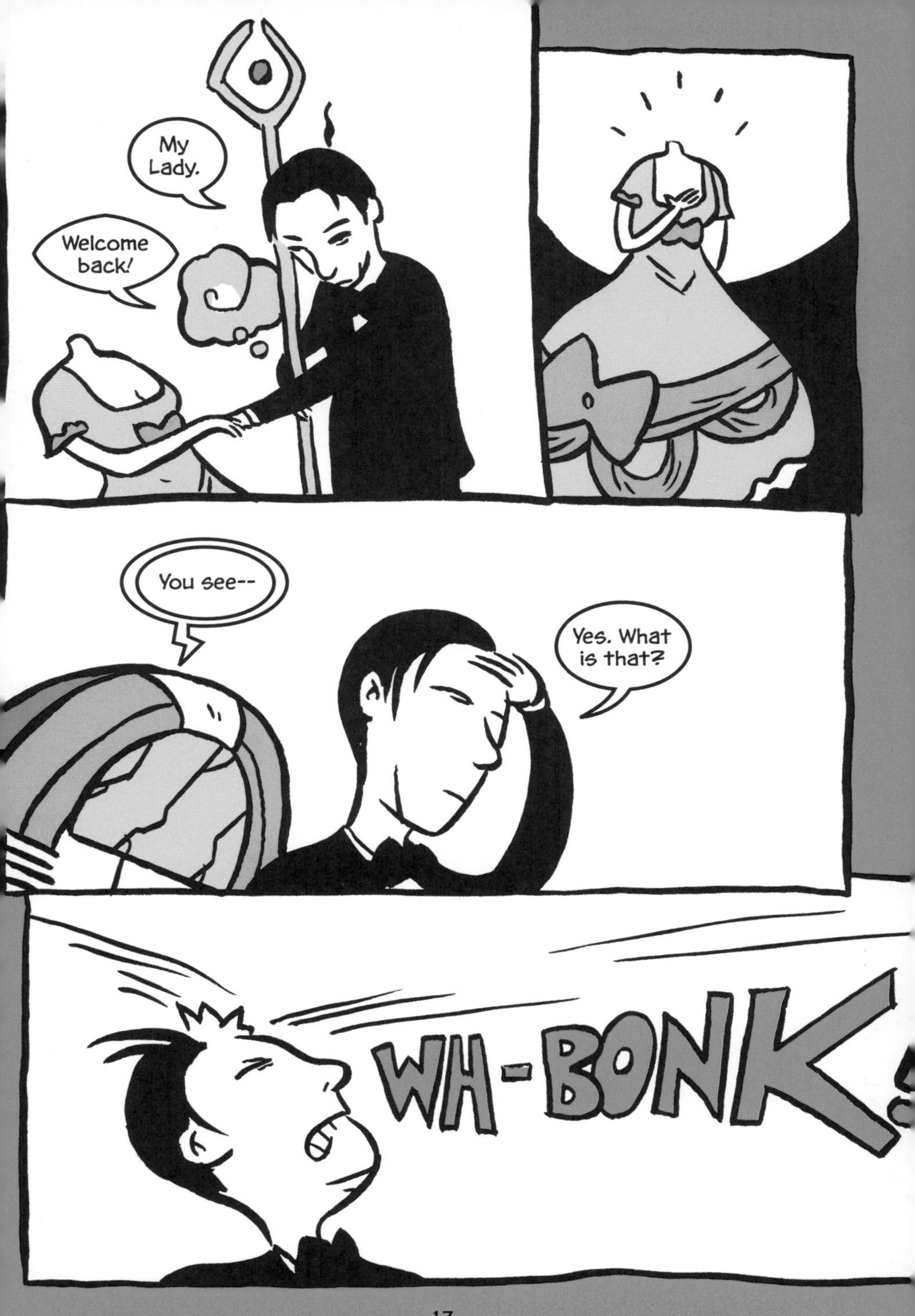
My Lady.
Welcome back!
You see--
Yes. What is that?
WH-BONK!

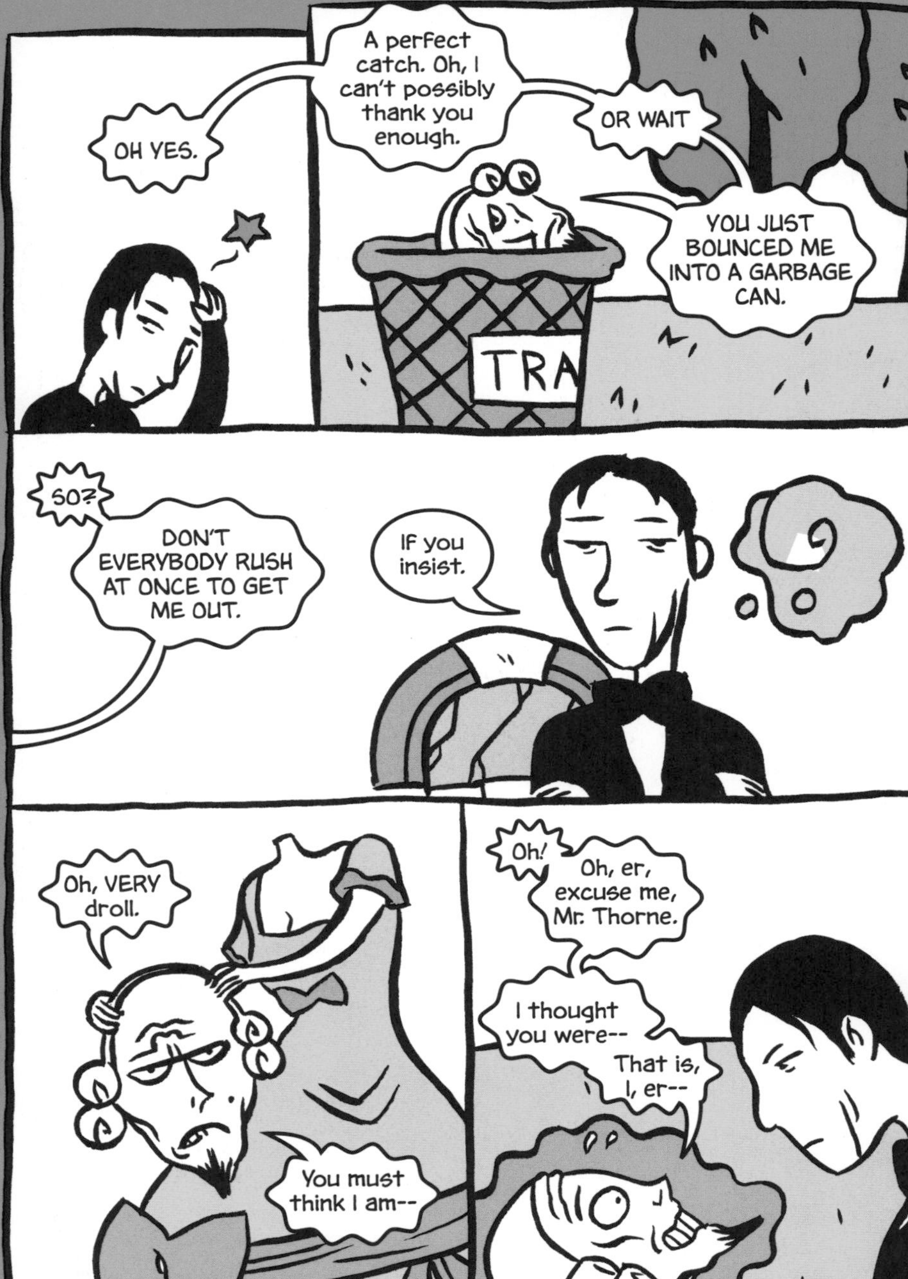
OH YES.
A perfect catch. Oh, I can't possibly thank you enough.
OR WAIT
YOU JUST BOUNCED ME INTO A GARBAGE CAN.
TRA
SO?
DON'T EVERYBODY RUSH AT ONCE TO GET ME OUT.
If you insist.
Oh, VERY droll.
You must think I am--
Oh!
Oh, er, excuse me, Mr. Thorne.
I thought you were--
That is, I, er--
ahem.

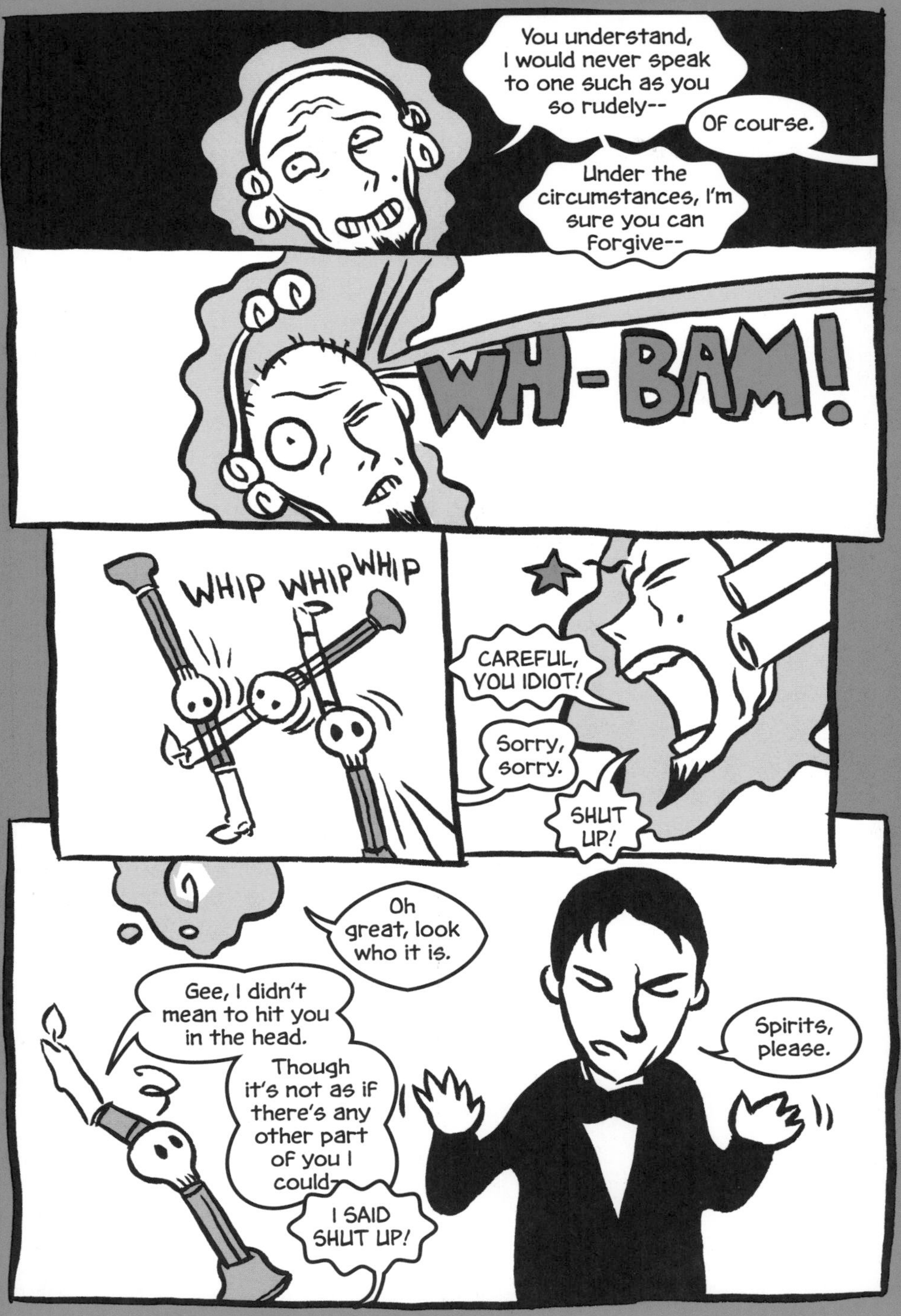
You understand, I would never speak to one such as you so rudely--
Of course.
Under the circumstances, I'm sure you can forgive--
WH-BAM!
WHIP WHIP WHIP
CAREFUL, YOU IDIOT!
Sorry, sorry.
SHUT UP!
Oh great, look who it is.
Gee, I didn't mean to hit you in the head.
Though it's not as if there's any other part of you I could--
I SAID SHUT UP!
Spirits, please.

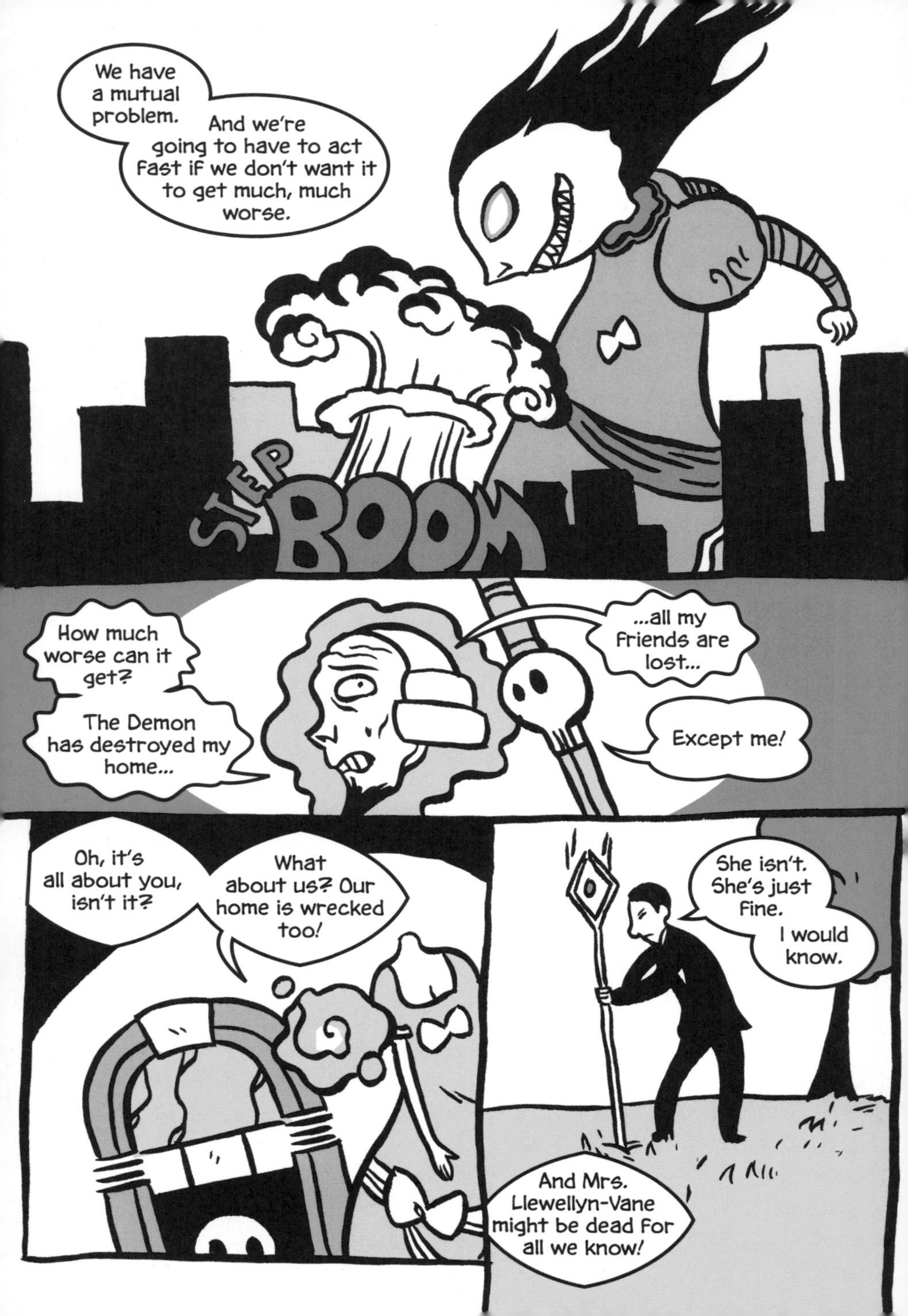

We have a mutual problem.
And we're going to have to act fast if we don't want it to get much, much worse.
STEP
BOOM
How much worse can it get?
The Demon has destroyed my home...
...all my friends are lost...
Except me!
Oh, it's all about you, isn't it?
What about us? Our home is wrecked too!
And Mrs. Llewellyn-Vane might be dead for all we know!
She isn't. She's just fine.
I would know.

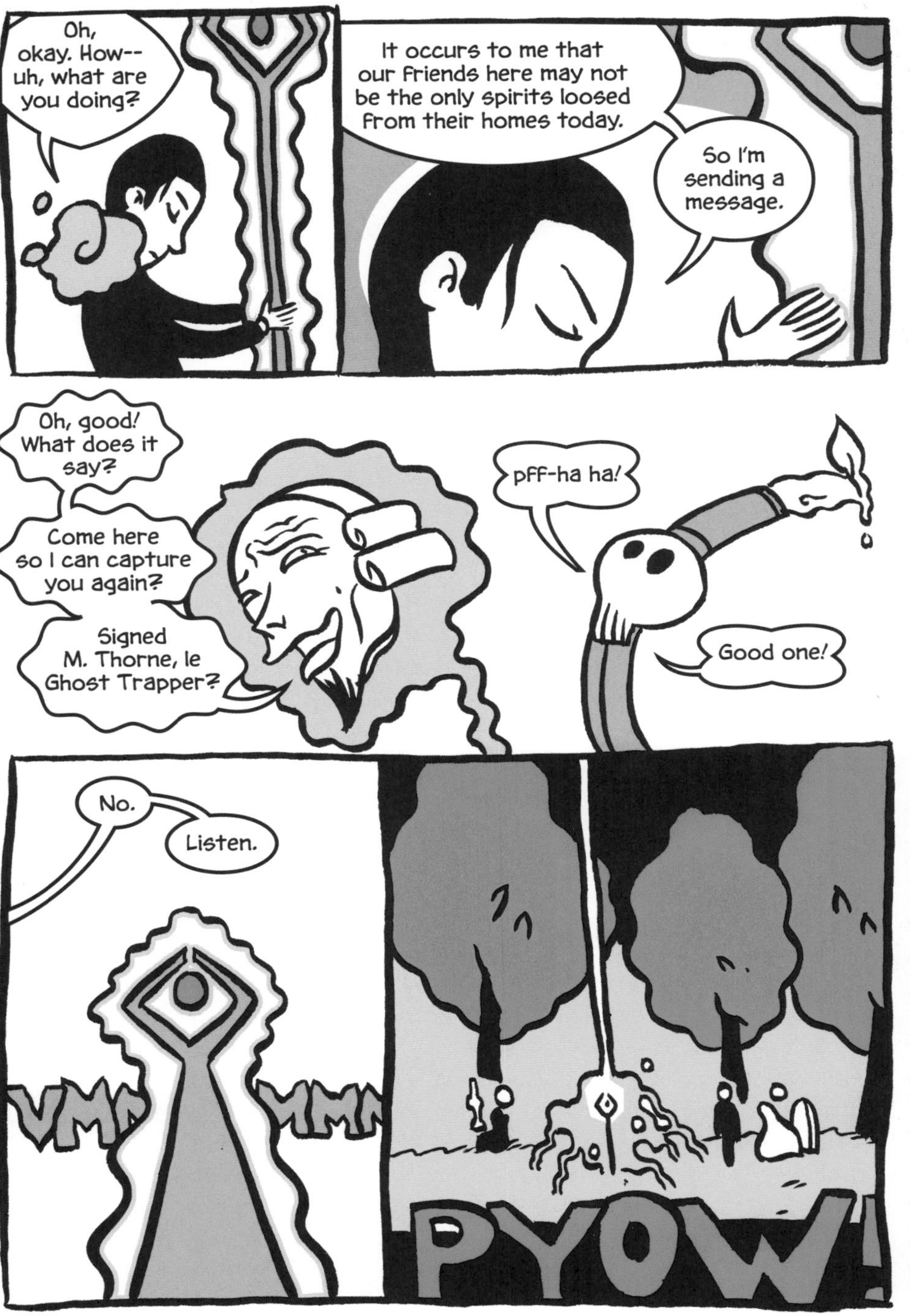

Oh, okay. How-- uh, what are you doing?
It occurs to me that our friends here may not be the only spirits loosed from their homes today.
So I'm sending a message.
Oh, good! What does it say?
Come here so I can capture you again?
Signed M. Thorne, le Ghost Trapper?
pff-ha ha!
Good one!
No.
Listen.
VMMMMM
PYOW!

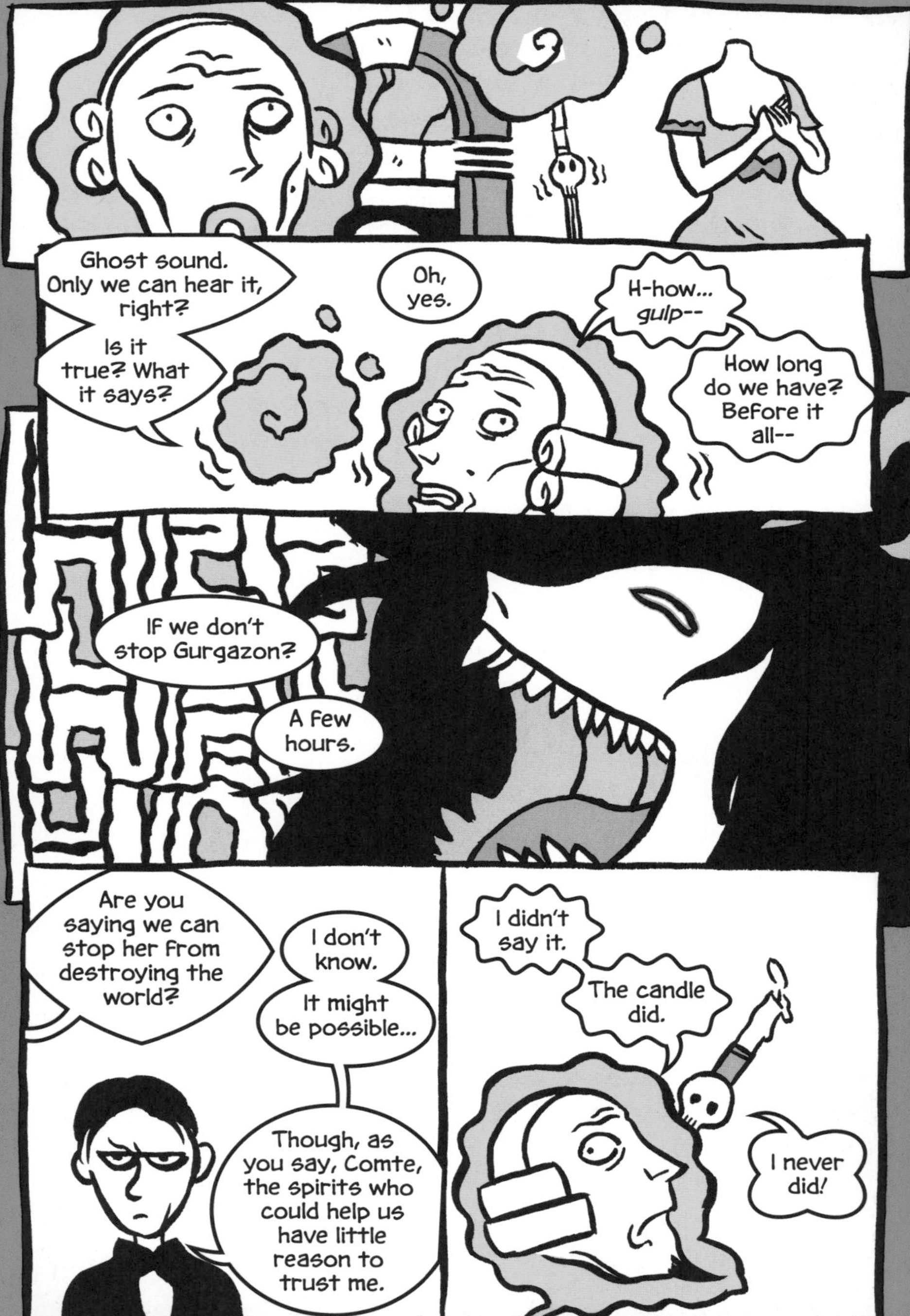

Ghost sound. Only we can hear it, right?
Is it true? What it says?
Oh, yes.
H-how... *gulp*--
How long do we have? Before it all--
If we don't stop Gurgazon?
A few hours.
Are you saying we can stop her from destroying the world?
I don't know.
It might be possible...
Though, as you say, Comte, the spirits who could help us have little reason to trust me.
I didn't say it.
The candle did.
I never did!

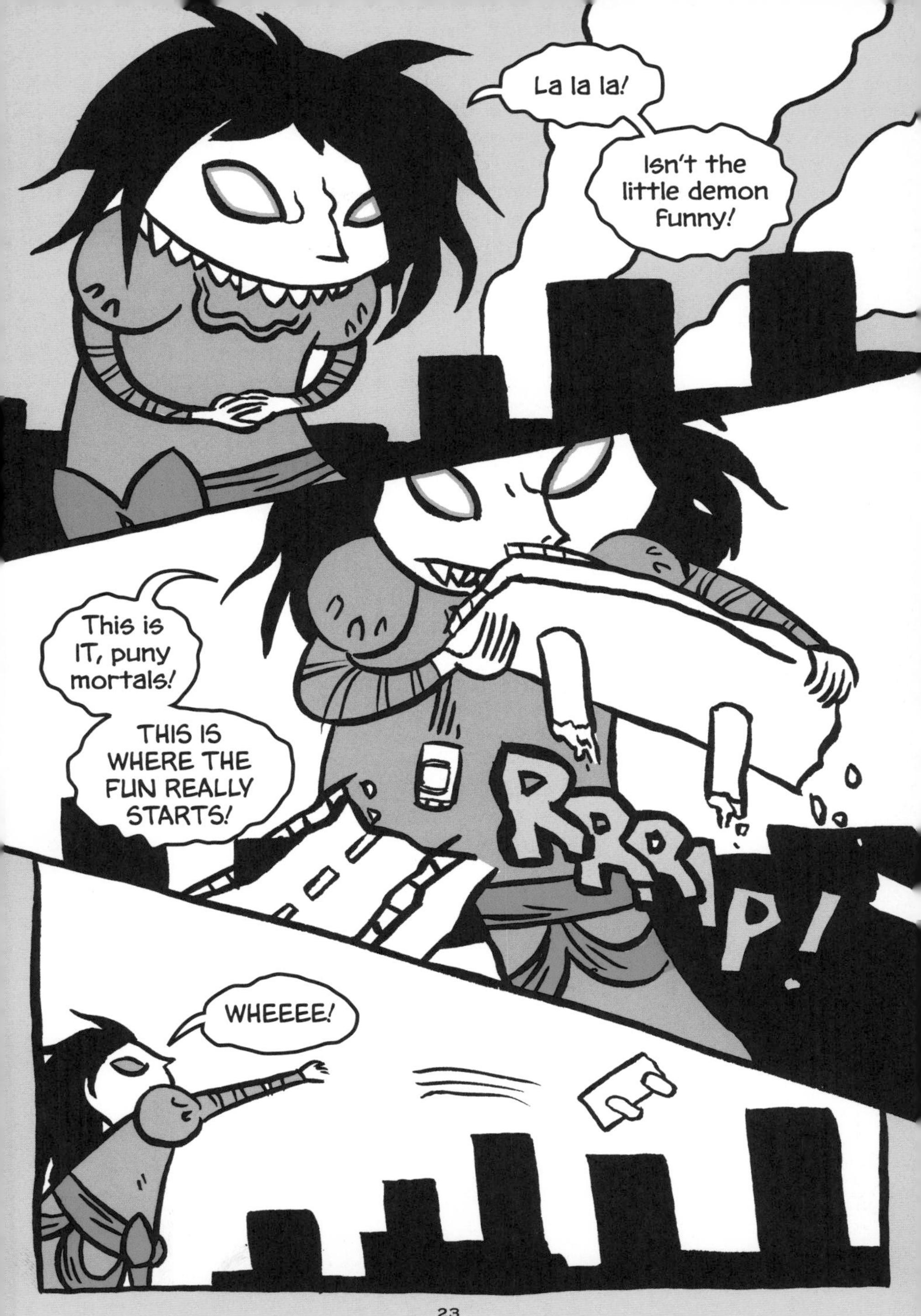
La la la!
Isn't the little demon funny!
This is IT, puny mortals!
THIS IS WHERE THE FUN REALLY STARTS!
RRRIP!
WHEEEE!

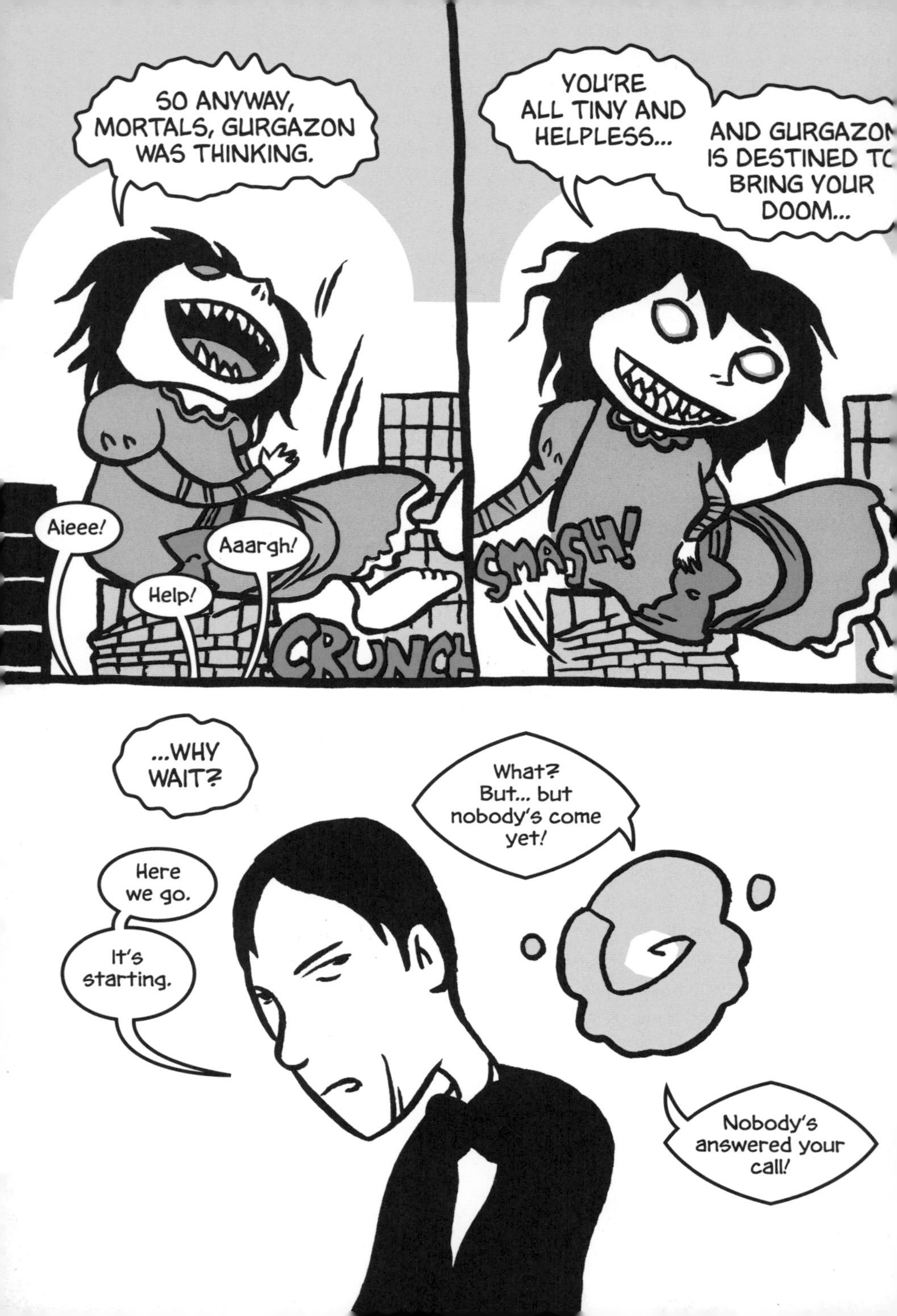
SO ANYWAY, MORTALS, GURGAZON WAS THINKING.
Aieee!
Help!
Aaargh!
CRUNCH
YOU'RE ALL TINY AND HELPLESS...
AND GURGAZON IS DESTINED TO BRING YOUR DOOM...
SMASH!
...WHY WAIT?
What? But... but nobody's come yet!
Here we go.
It's starting.
Nobody's answered your call!

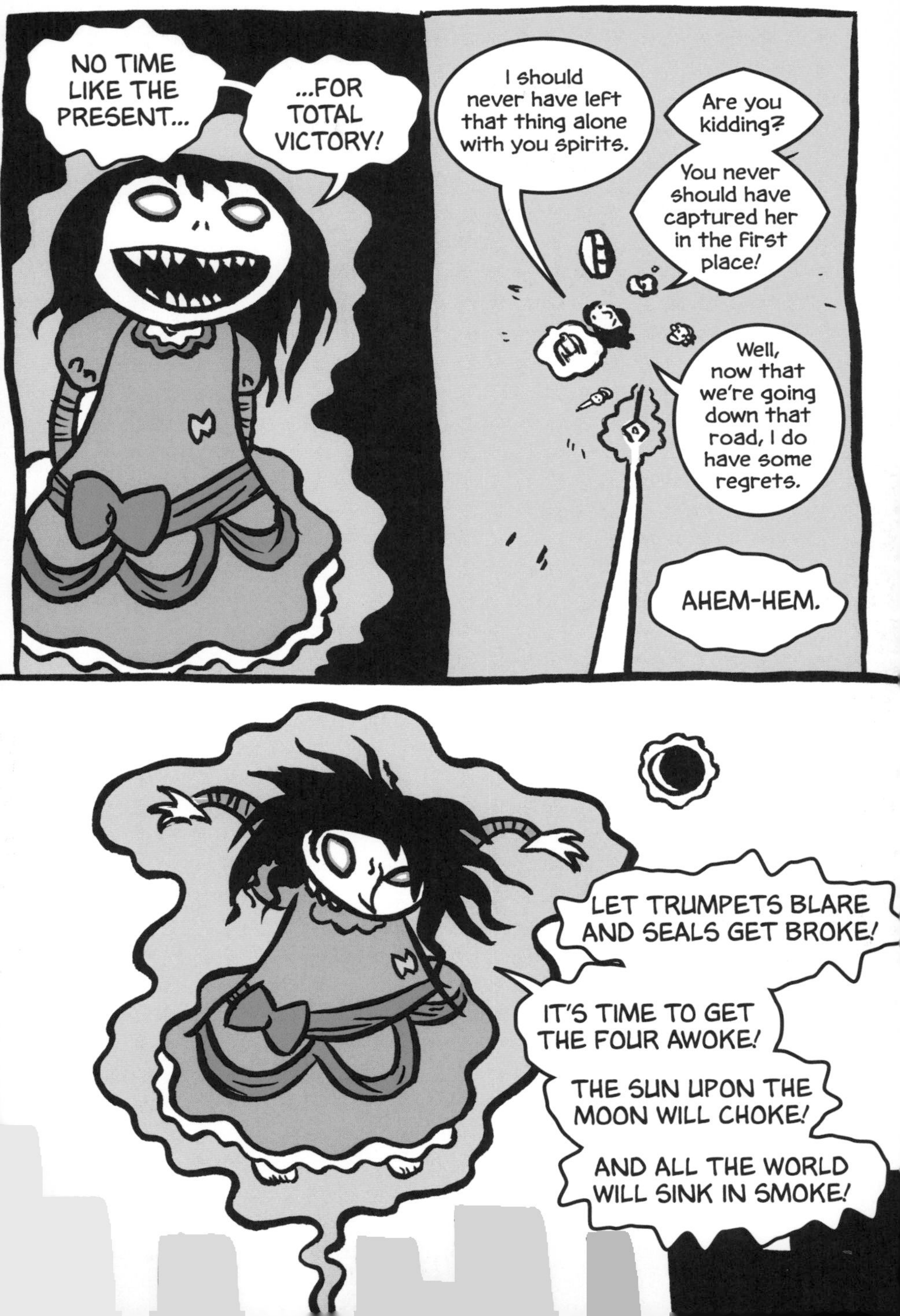

NO TIME LIKE THE PRESENT...
...FOR TOTAL VICTORY!
I should never have left that thing alone with you spirits.
Are you kidding?
You never should have captured her in the first place!
Well, now that we're going down that road, I do have some regrets.
AHEM-HEM.
LET TRUMPETS BLARE AND SEALS GET BROKE!
IT'S TIME TO GET THE FOUR AWOKE!
THE SUN UPON THE MOON WILL CHOKE!
AND ALL THE WORLD WILL SINK IN SMOKE!

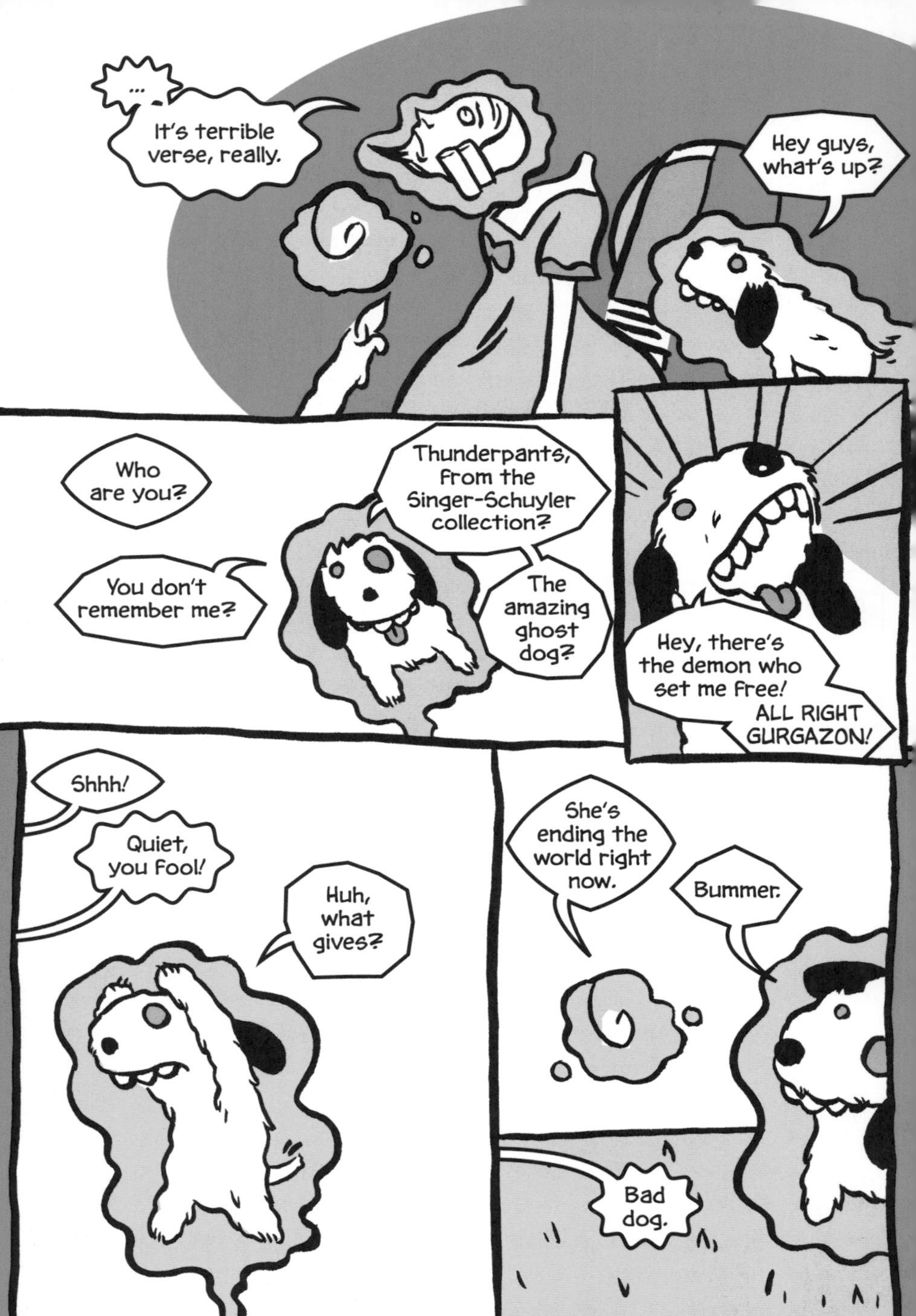
...
It's terrible verse, really.
Hey guys, what's up?
Who are you?
Thunderpants, from the Singer-Schuyler collection?
You don't remember me?
The amazing ghost dog?
Hey, there's the demon who set me free!
ALL RIGHT GURGAZON!
Shhh!
Quiet, you fool!
Huh, what gives?
She's ending the world right now.
Bummer.
Bad dog.

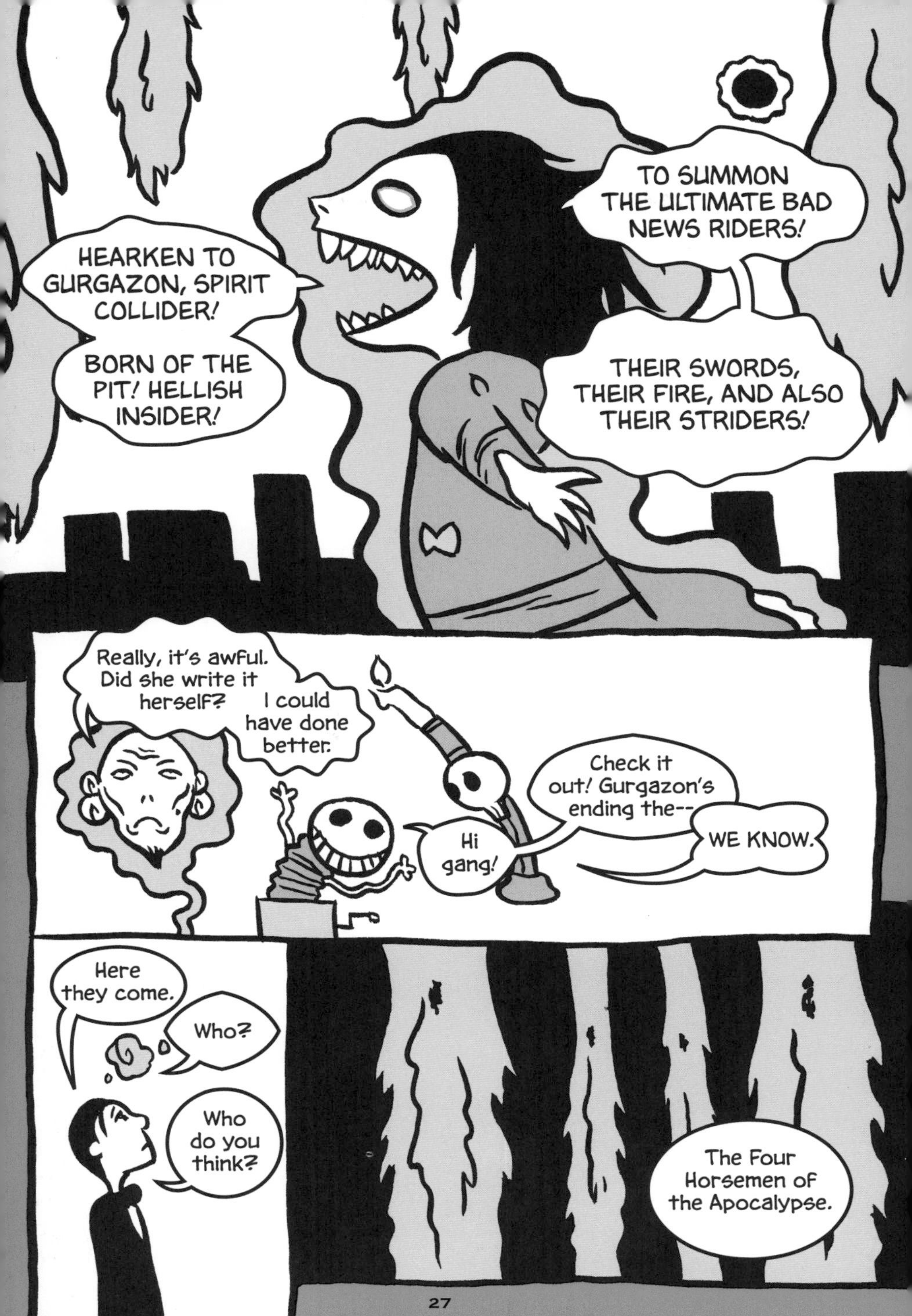
HEARKEN TO GURGAZON, SPIRIT COLLIDER!
BORN OF THE PIT! HELLISH INSIDER!
TO SUMMON THE ULTIMATE BAD NEWS RIDERS!
THEIR SWORDS, THEIR FIRE, AND ALSO THEIR STRIDERS!
Really, it's awful. Did she write it herself?
I could have done better.
Check it out! Gurgazon's ending the--
WE KNOW.
Hi gang!
Here they come.
Who?
Who do you think?
The Four Horsemen of the Apocalypse.

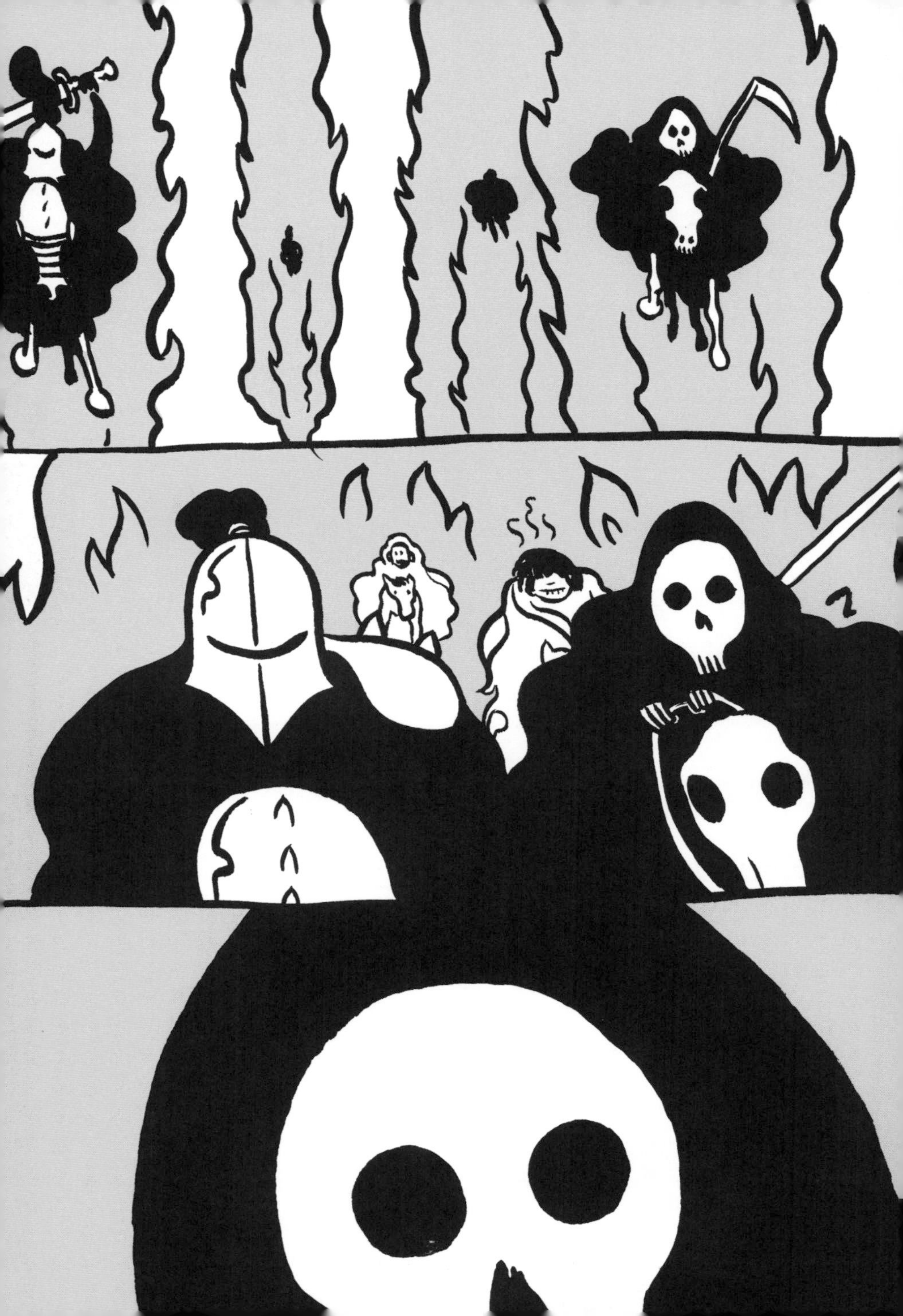

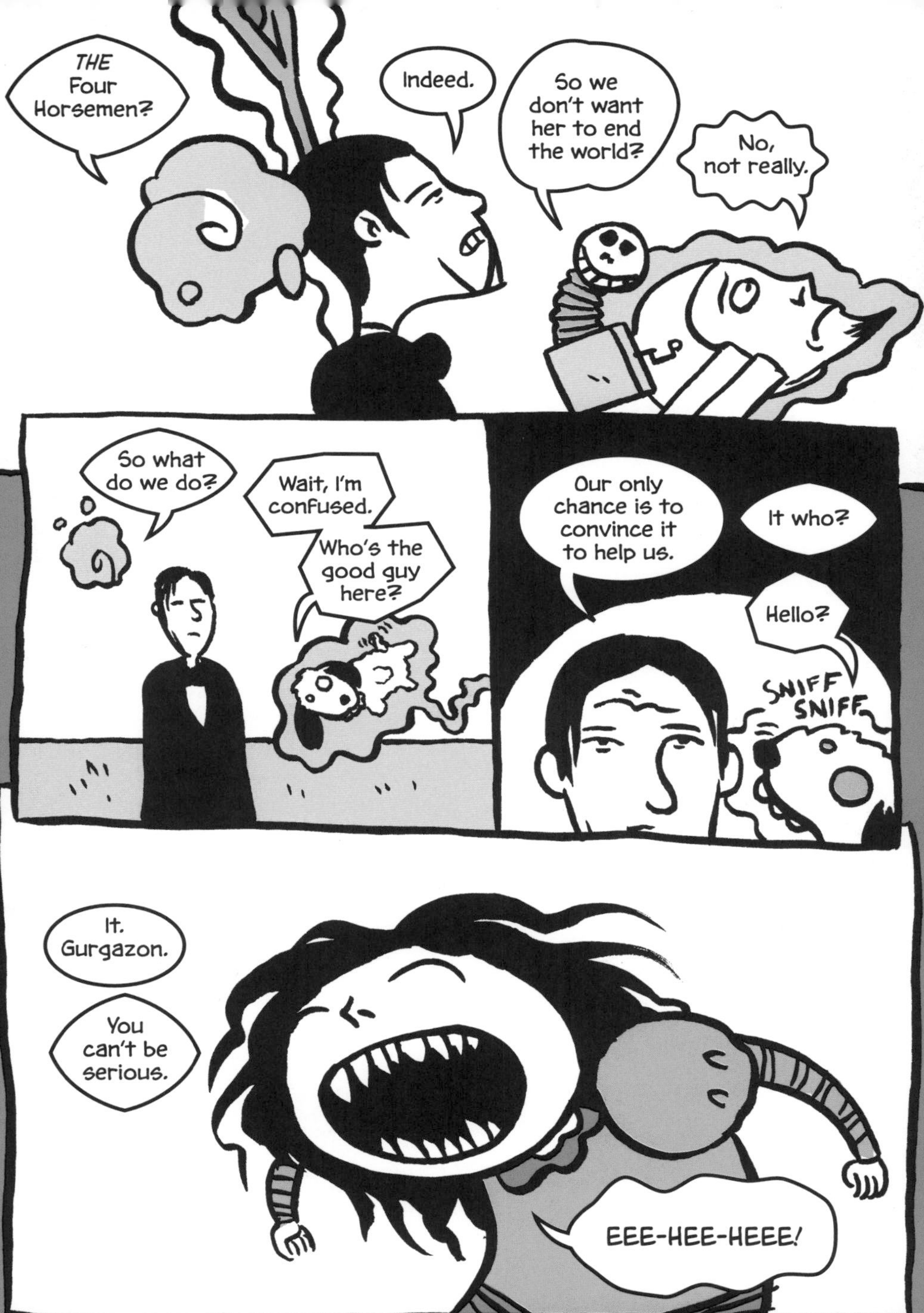
THE Four Horsemen?
Indeed.
So we don't want her to end the world?
No, not really.
So what do we do?
Wait, I'm confused.
Who's the good guy here?
Our only chance is to convince it to help us.
It who?
Hello?
SNIFF SNIFF
It. Gurgazon.
You can't be serious.
EEE-HEE-HEEE!

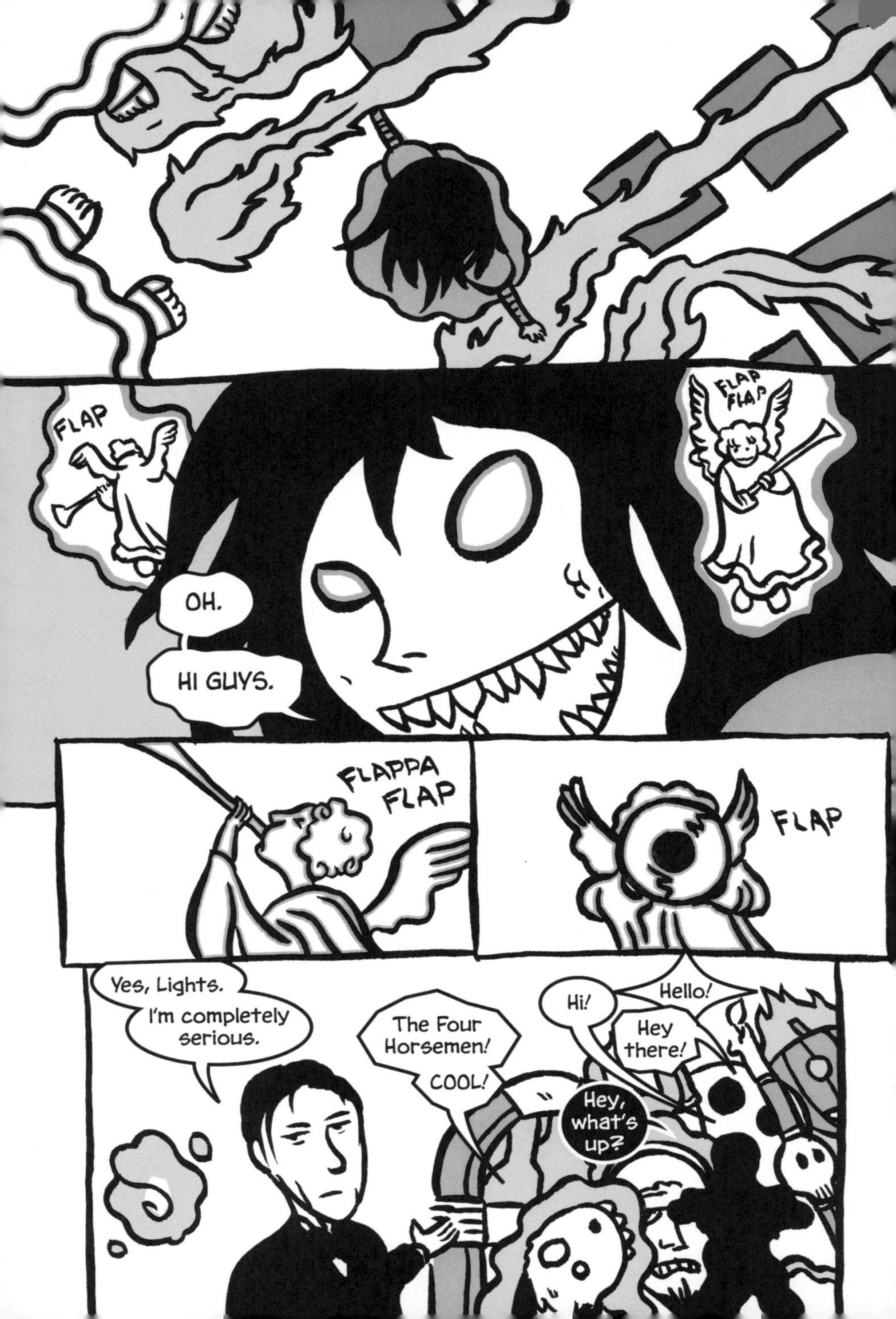
FLAP
FLAP FLAP
OH.
HI GUYS.
FLAPPA FLAP
FLAP
Yes, Lights.
I'm completely serious.
The Four Horsemen!
COOL!
Hi!
Hello!
Hey there!
Hey, what's up?

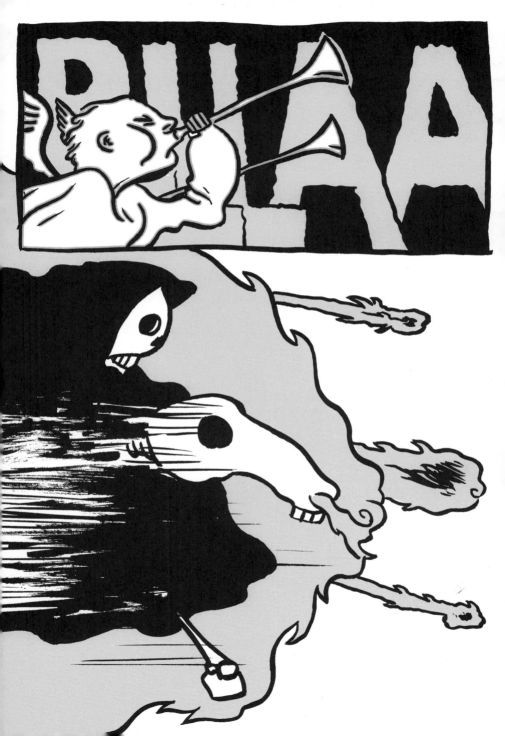

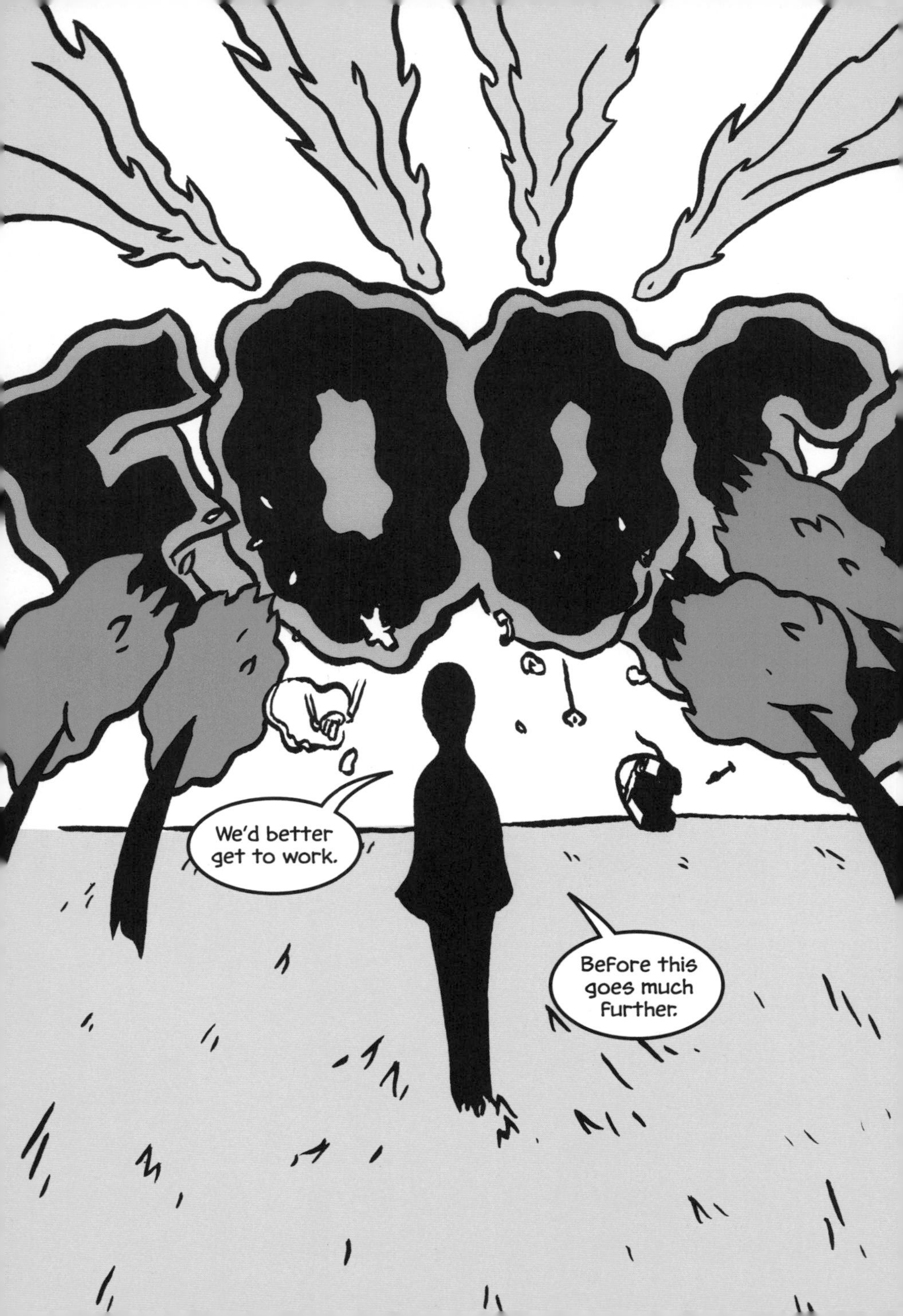

FOOOO
We'd better get to work.
Before this goes much further.

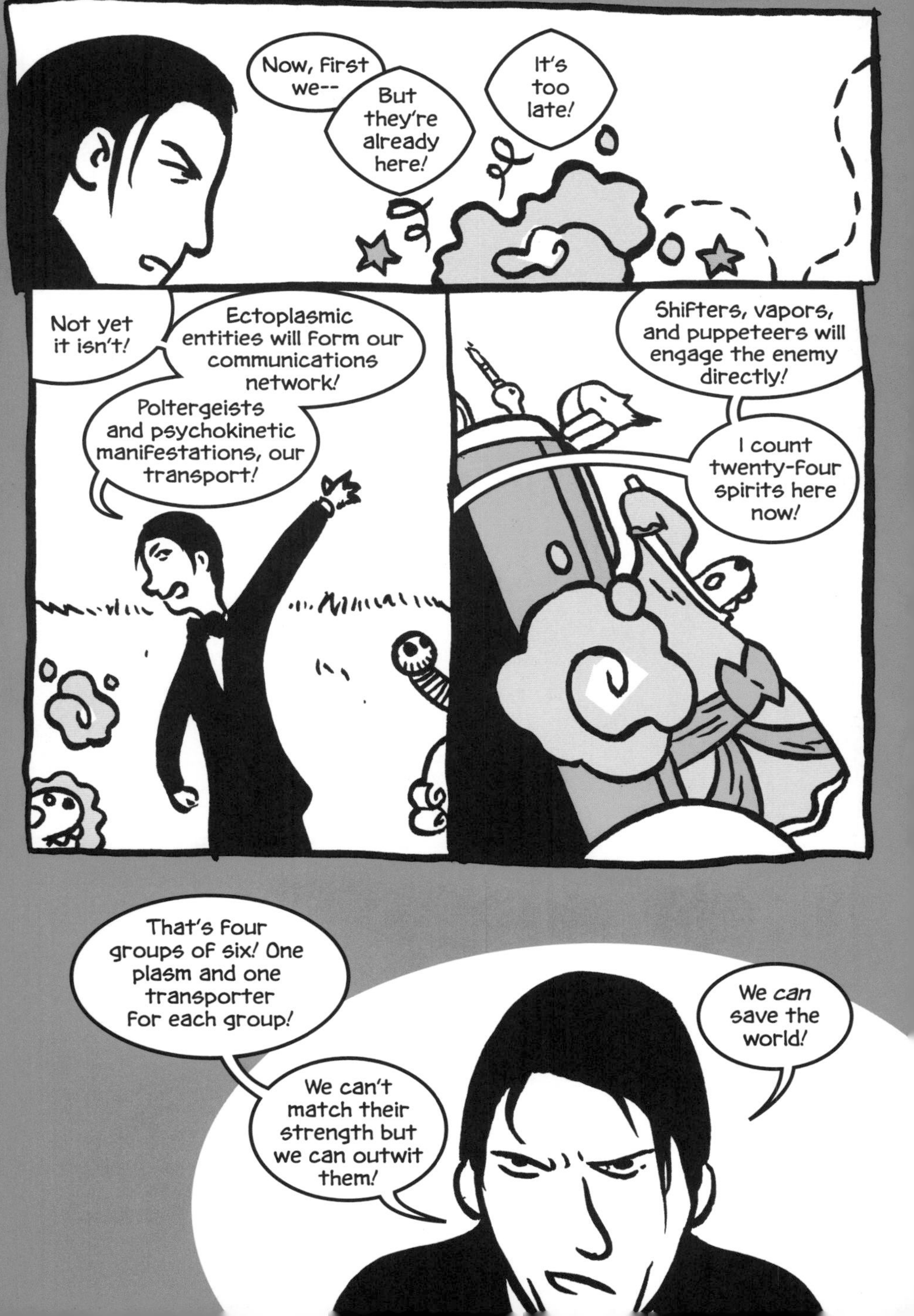
Now, first we--
But they're already here!
It's too late!
Not yet it isn't!
Ectoplasmic entities will form our communications network!
Poltergeists and psychokinetic manifestations, our transport!
Shifters, vapors, and puppeteers will engage the enemy directly!
I count twenty-four spirits here now!
That's four groups of six! One plasm and one transporter for each group!
We can't match their strength but we can outwit them!
We *can* save the world!

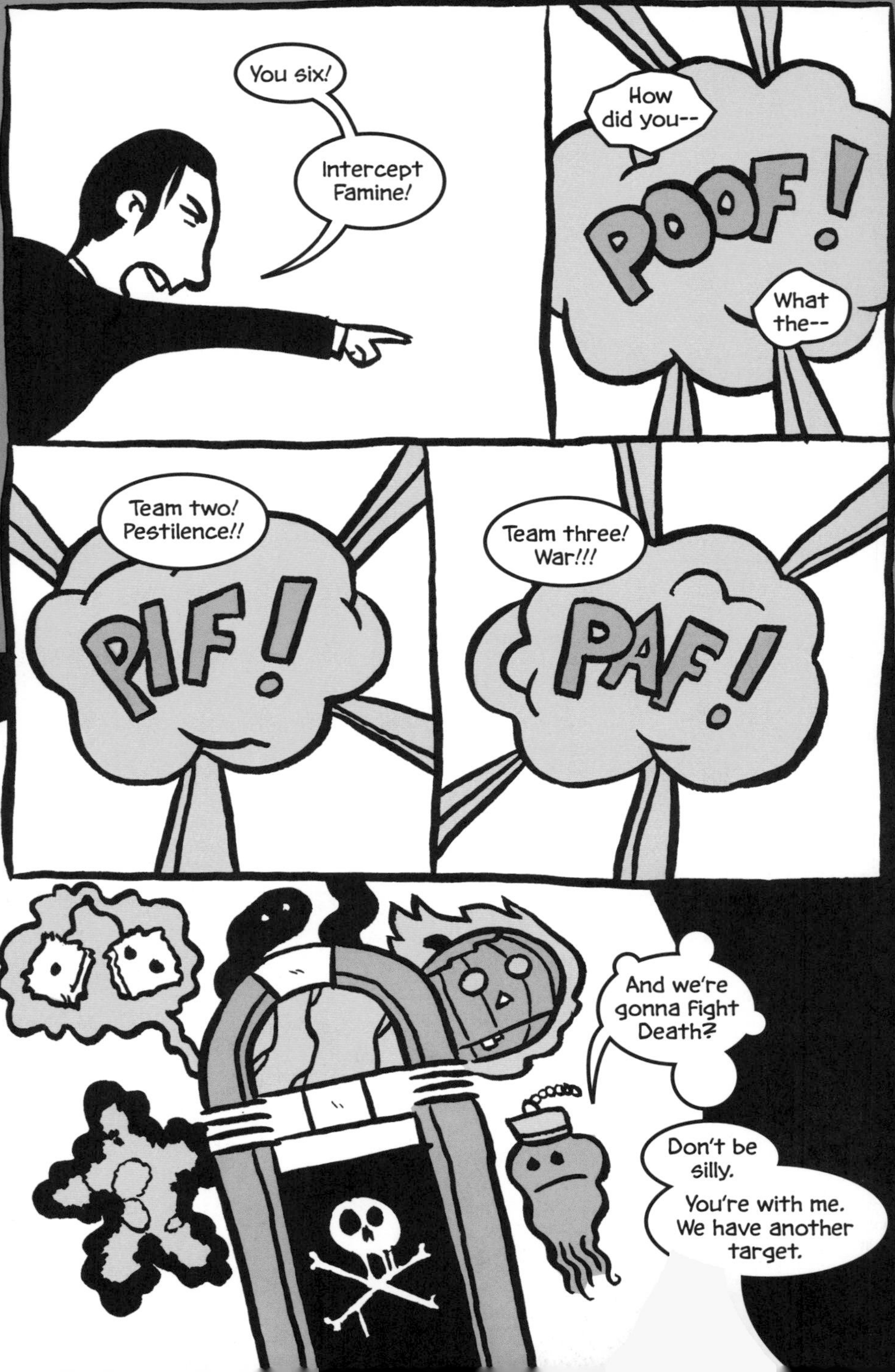
You six!
Intercept Famine!
How did you--
POOF!
What the--
Team two! Pestilence!!
PIF!
Team three! War!!!
PAF!
And we're gonna fight Death?
Don't be silly.
You're with me. We have another target.

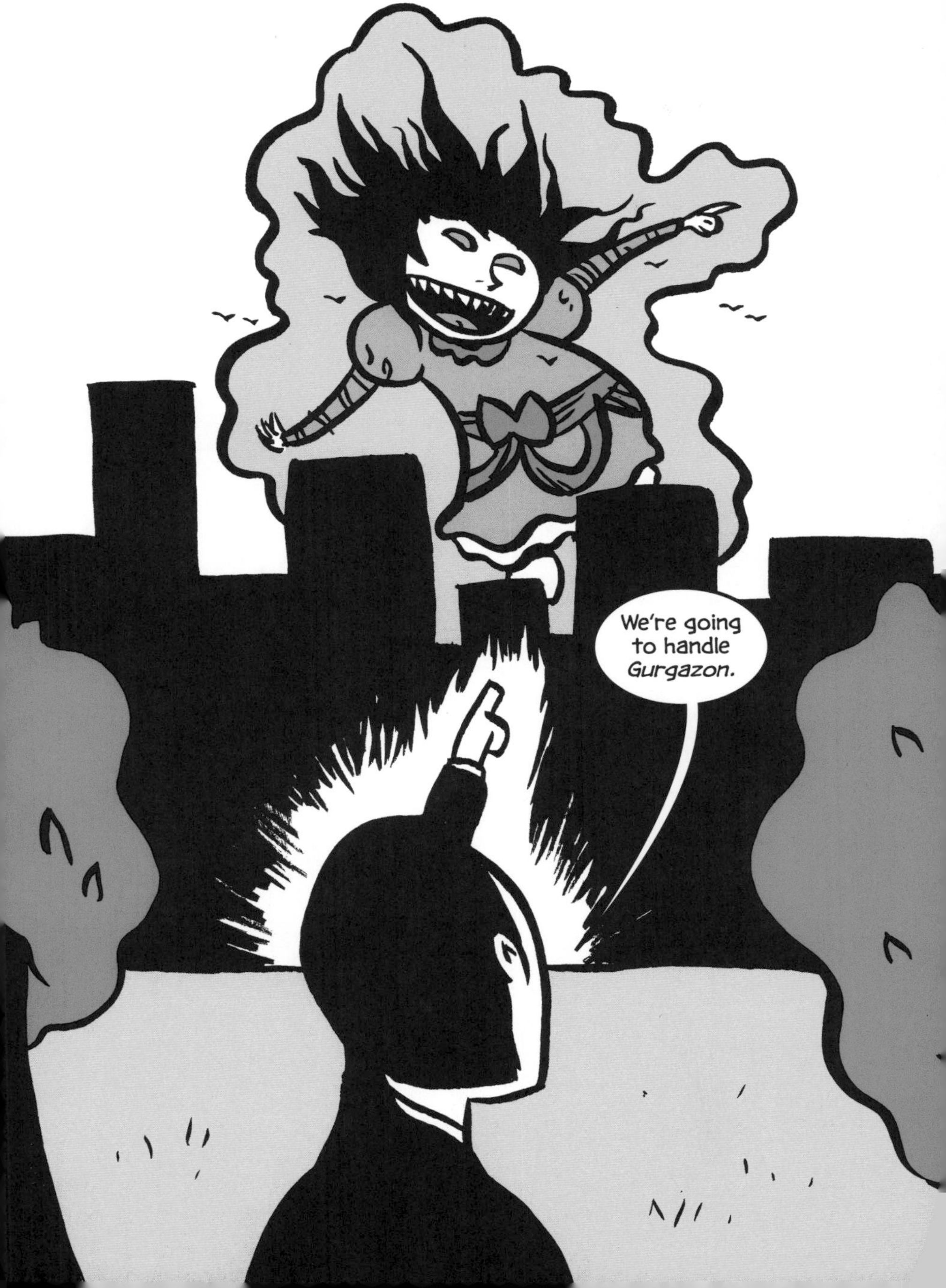
We're going to handle Gurgazon.

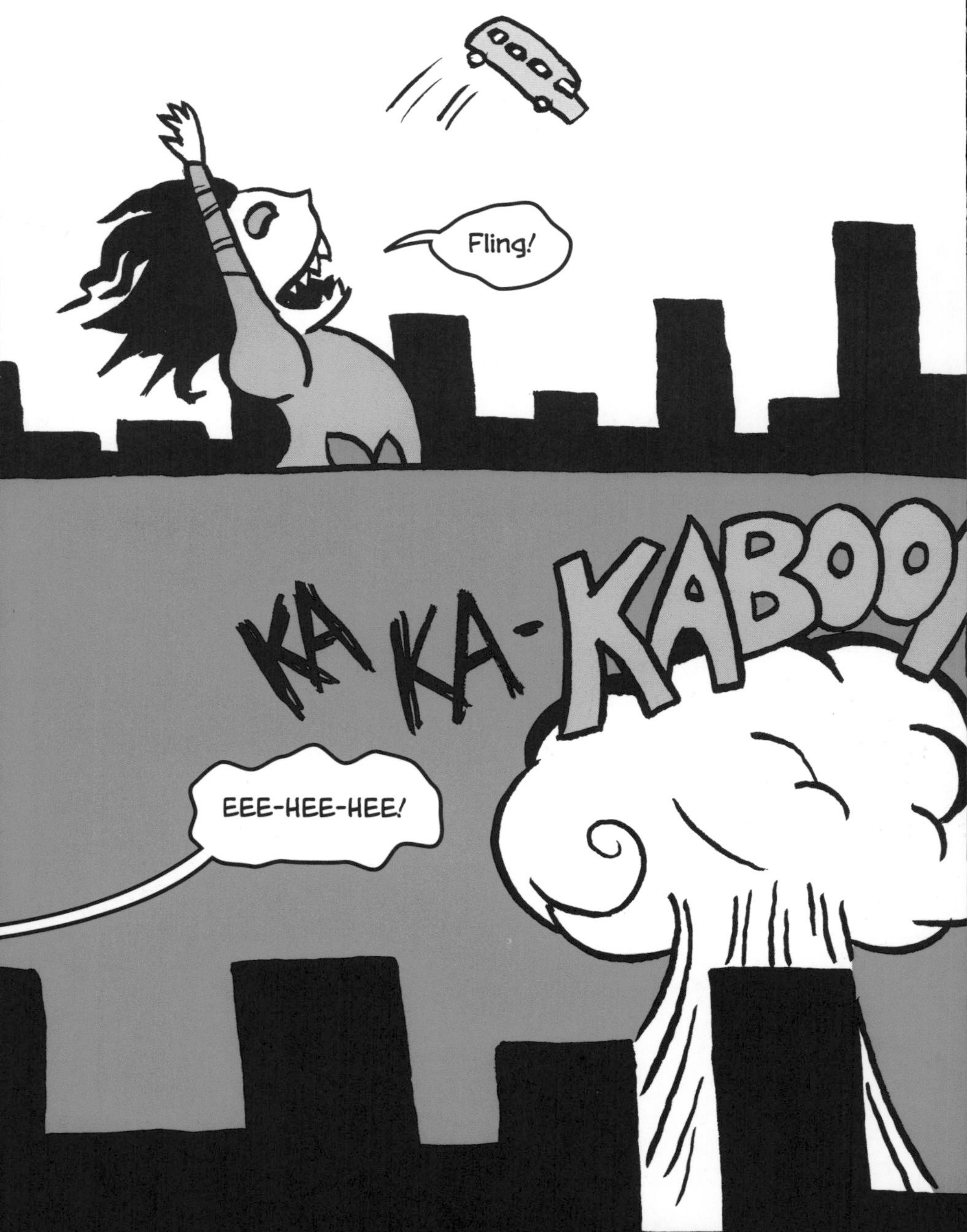
Fling!
KA KA-KABOO
EEE-HEE-HEE!

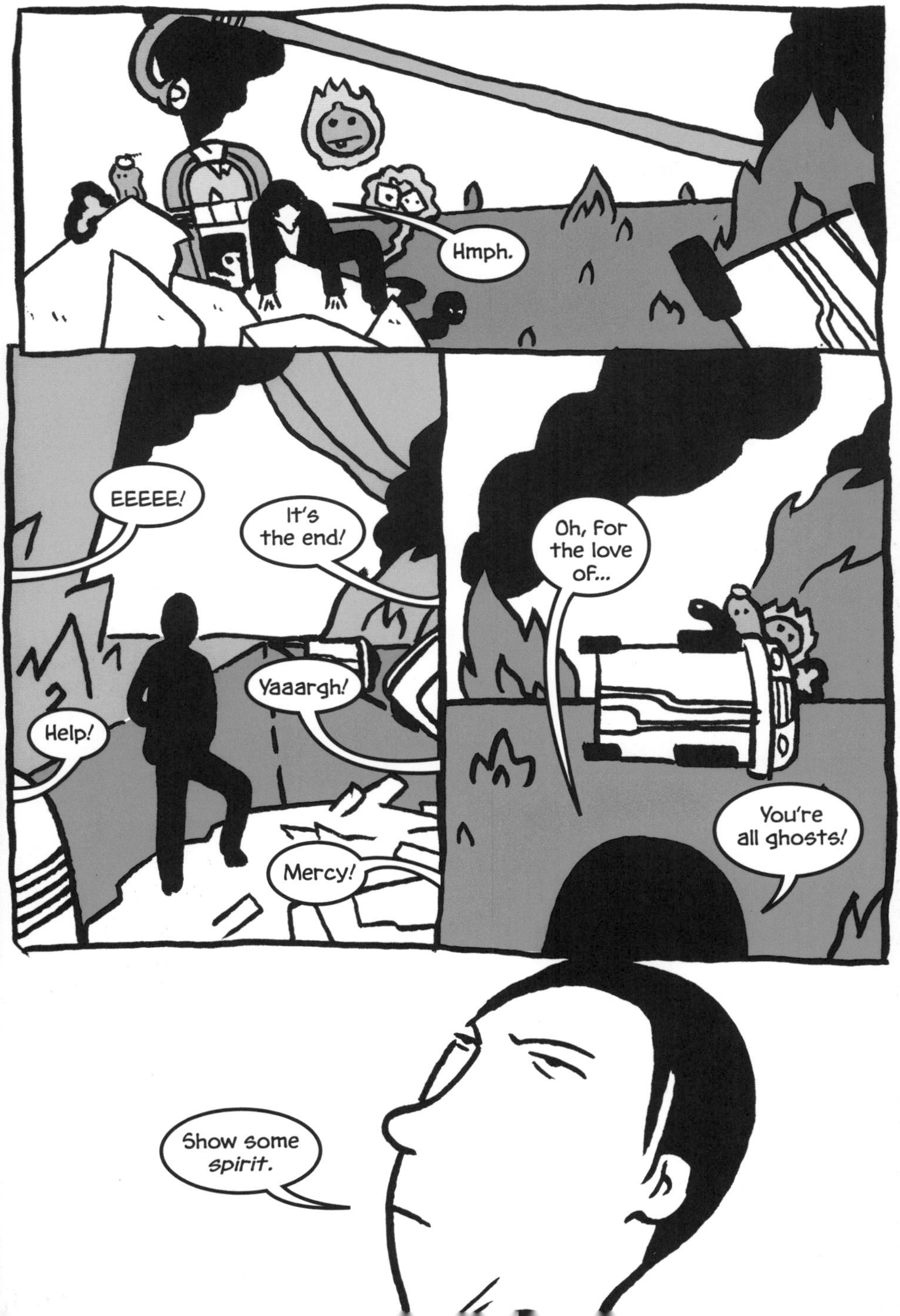
Hmph.
EEEEE!
It's the end!
Help!
Yaaargh!
Mercy!
Oh, for the love of...
You're all ghosts!
Show some spirit.

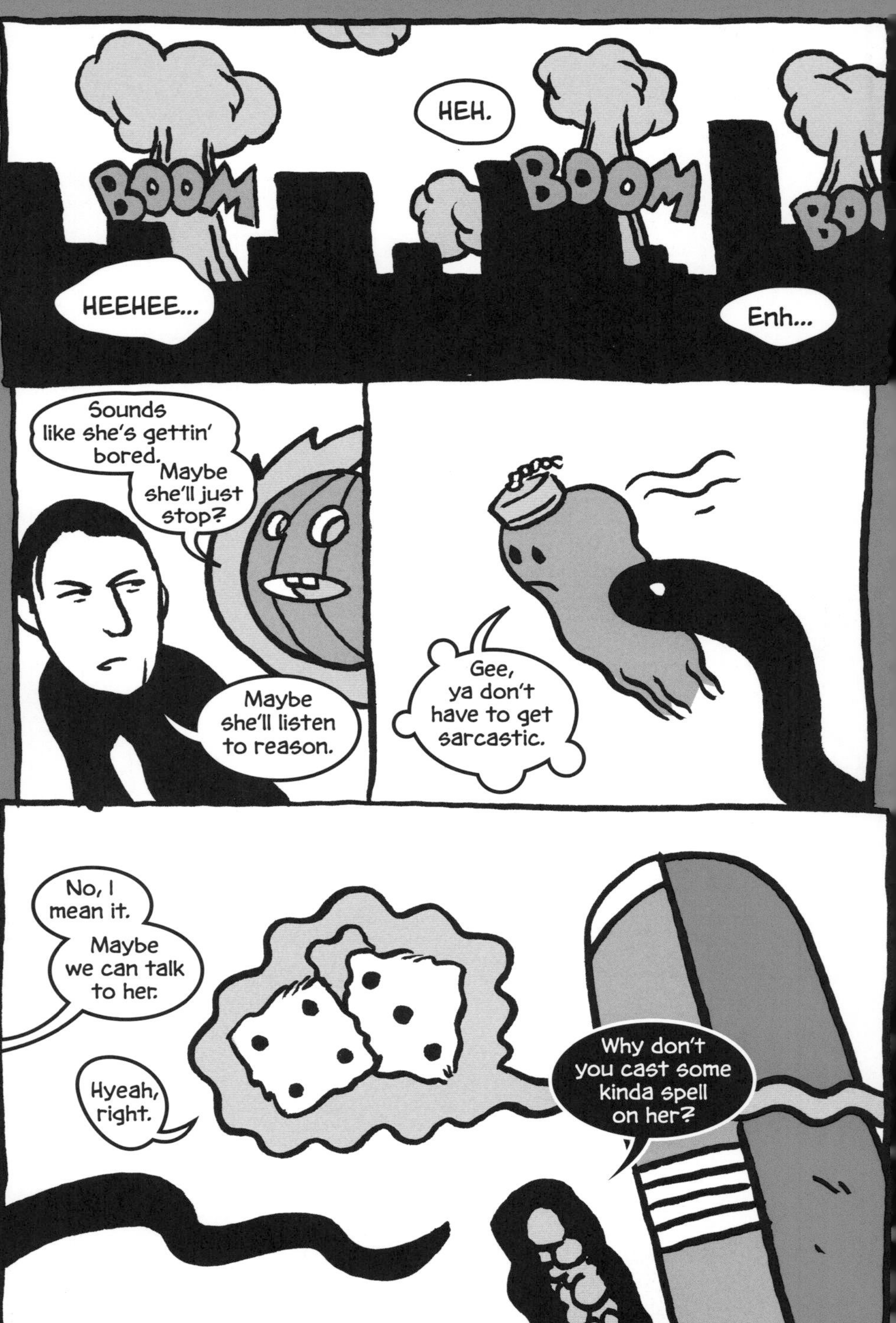
BOOM
HEH.
BOOM
BOO
HEEHEE...
Enh...
Sounds like she's gettin' bored.
Maybe she'll just stop?
Maybe she'll listen to reason.
Gee, ya don't have to get sarcastic.
No, I mean it.
Maybe we can talk to her.
Hyeah, right.
Why don't you cast some kinda spell on her?

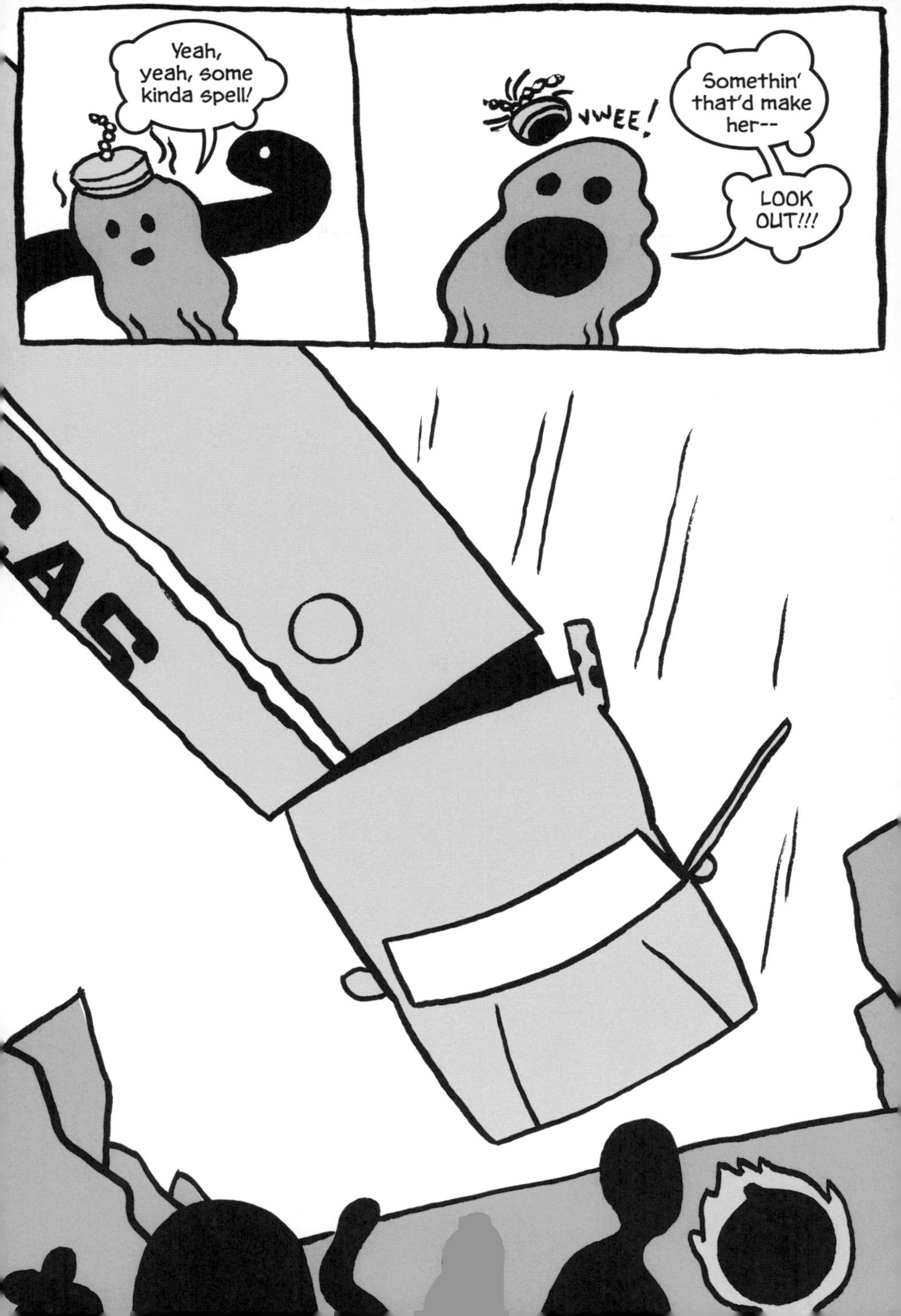
Yeah, yeah, some kinda spell!
VWEE!
Somethin' that'd make her--
LOOK OUT!!!
CAG

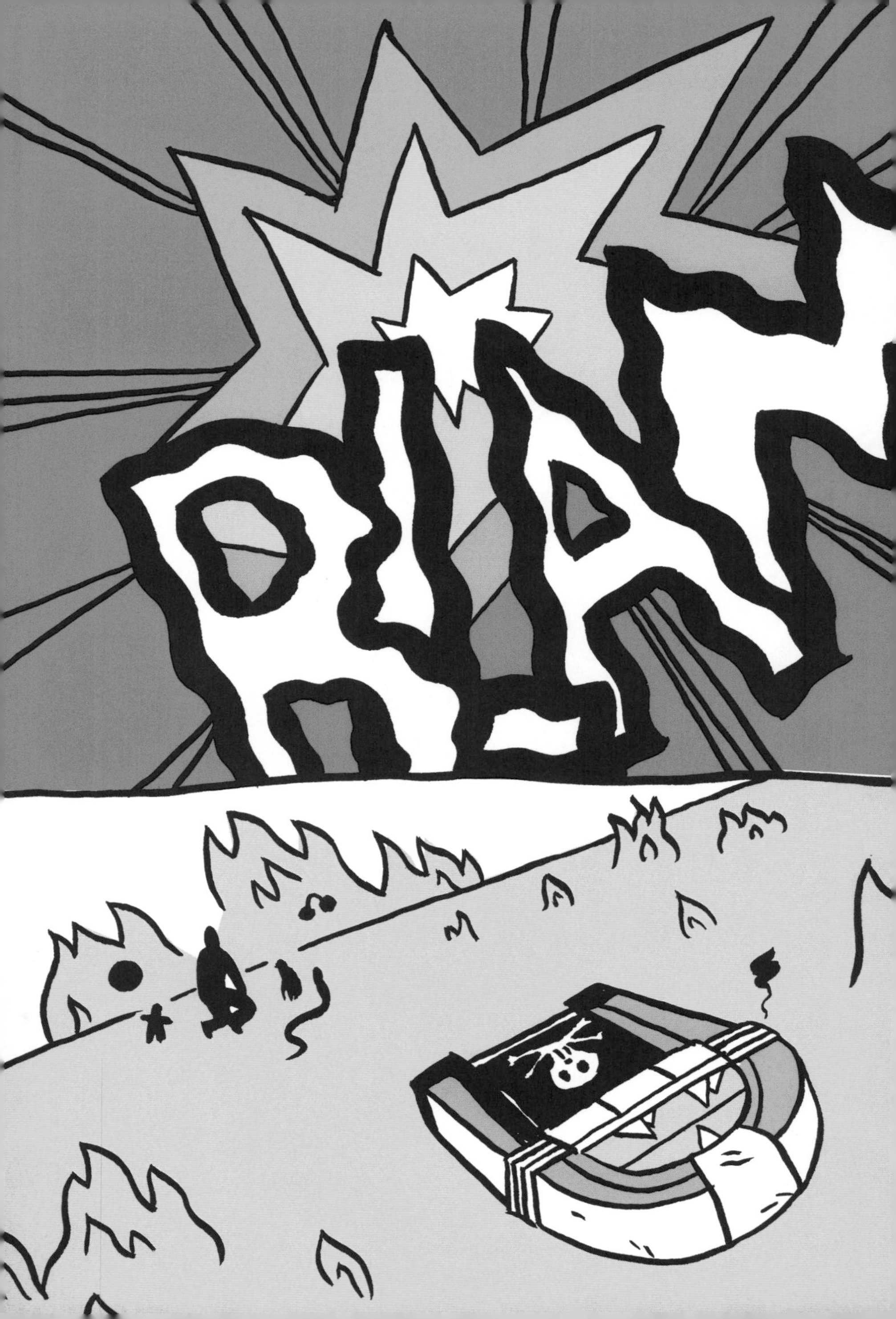

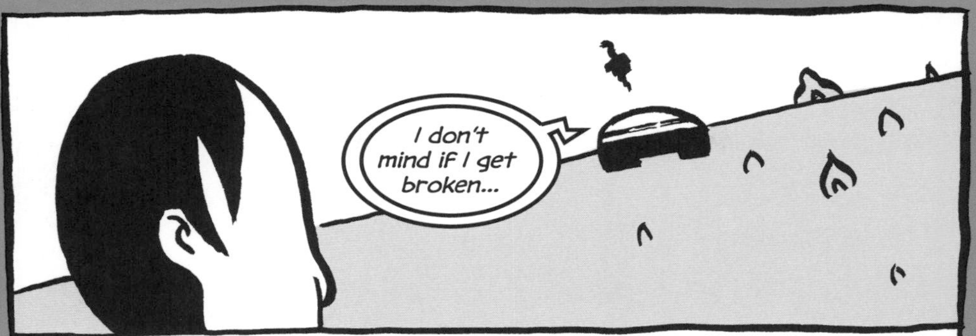
I don't mind if I get broken...

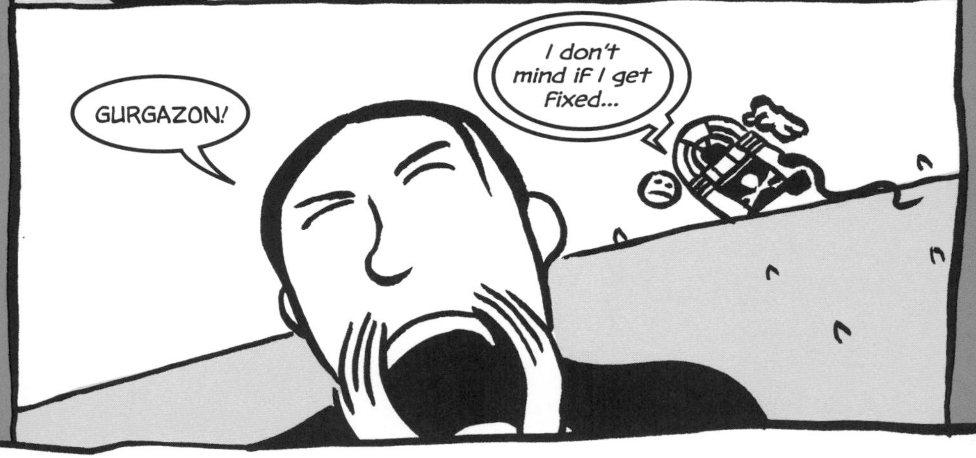
GURGAZON!
I don't mind if I get fixed...

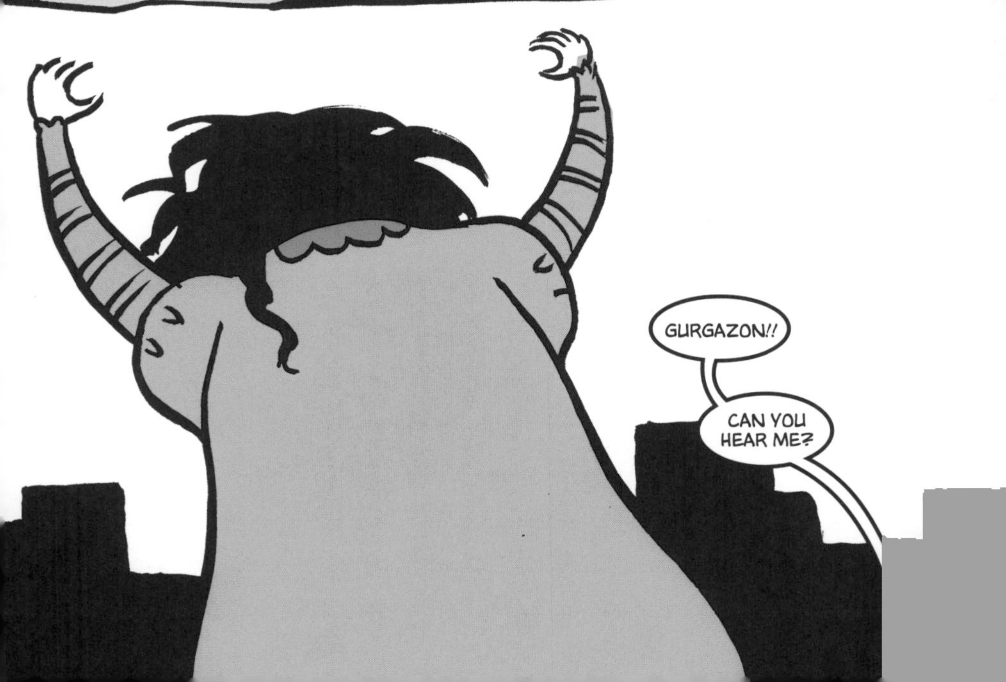
GURGAZON!!
CAN YOU HEAR ME?

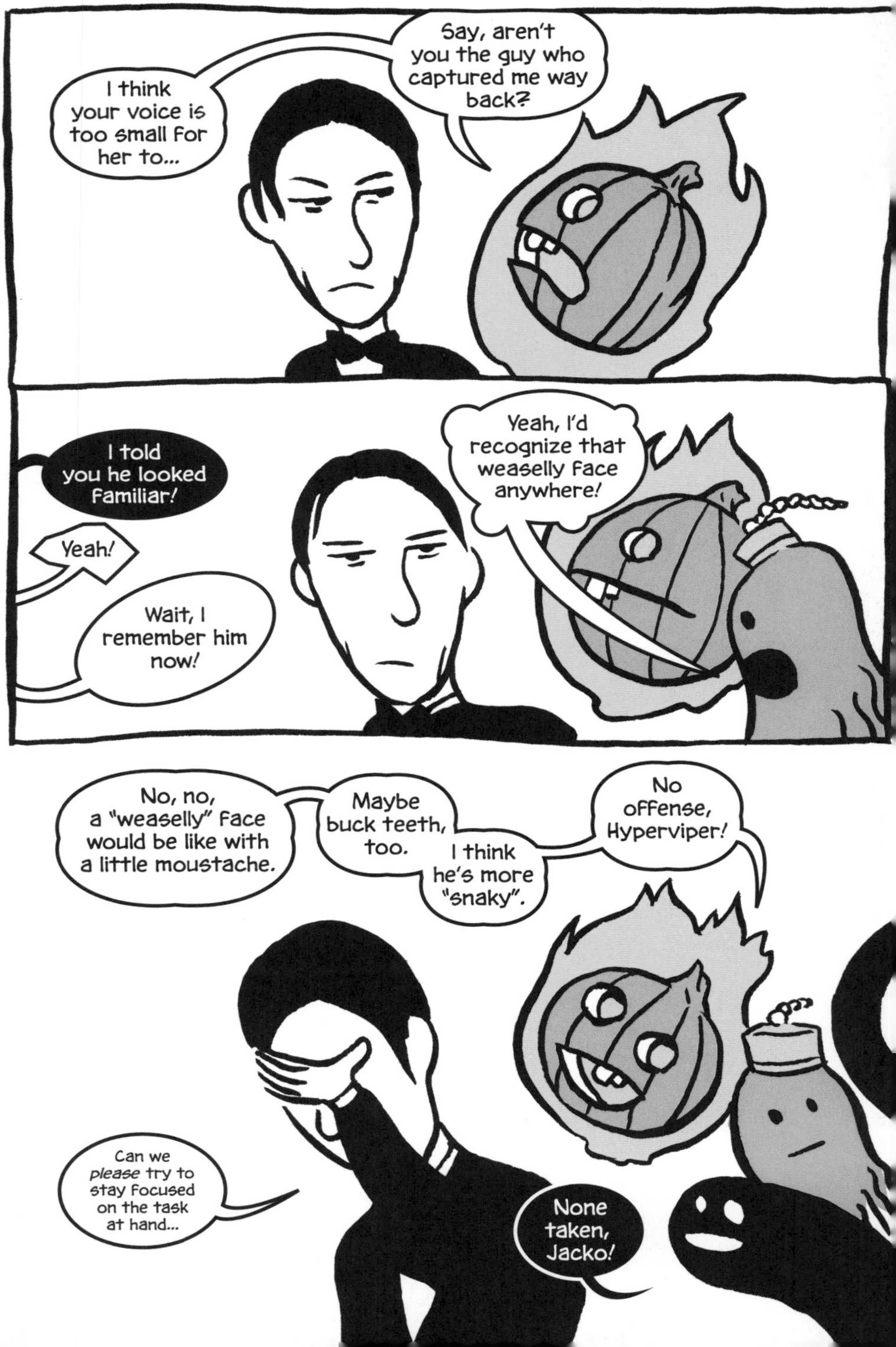
I think your voice is too small for her to...
Say, aren't you the guy who captured me way back?
I told you he looked familiar!
Yeah!
Wait, I remember him now!
Yeah, I'd recognize that weaselly face anywhere!
No, no, a "weaselly" face would be like with a little moustache.
Maybe buck teeth, too.
I think he's more "snaky".
No offense, Hyperviper!
Can we *please* try to stay focused on the task at hand...
None taken, Jacko!

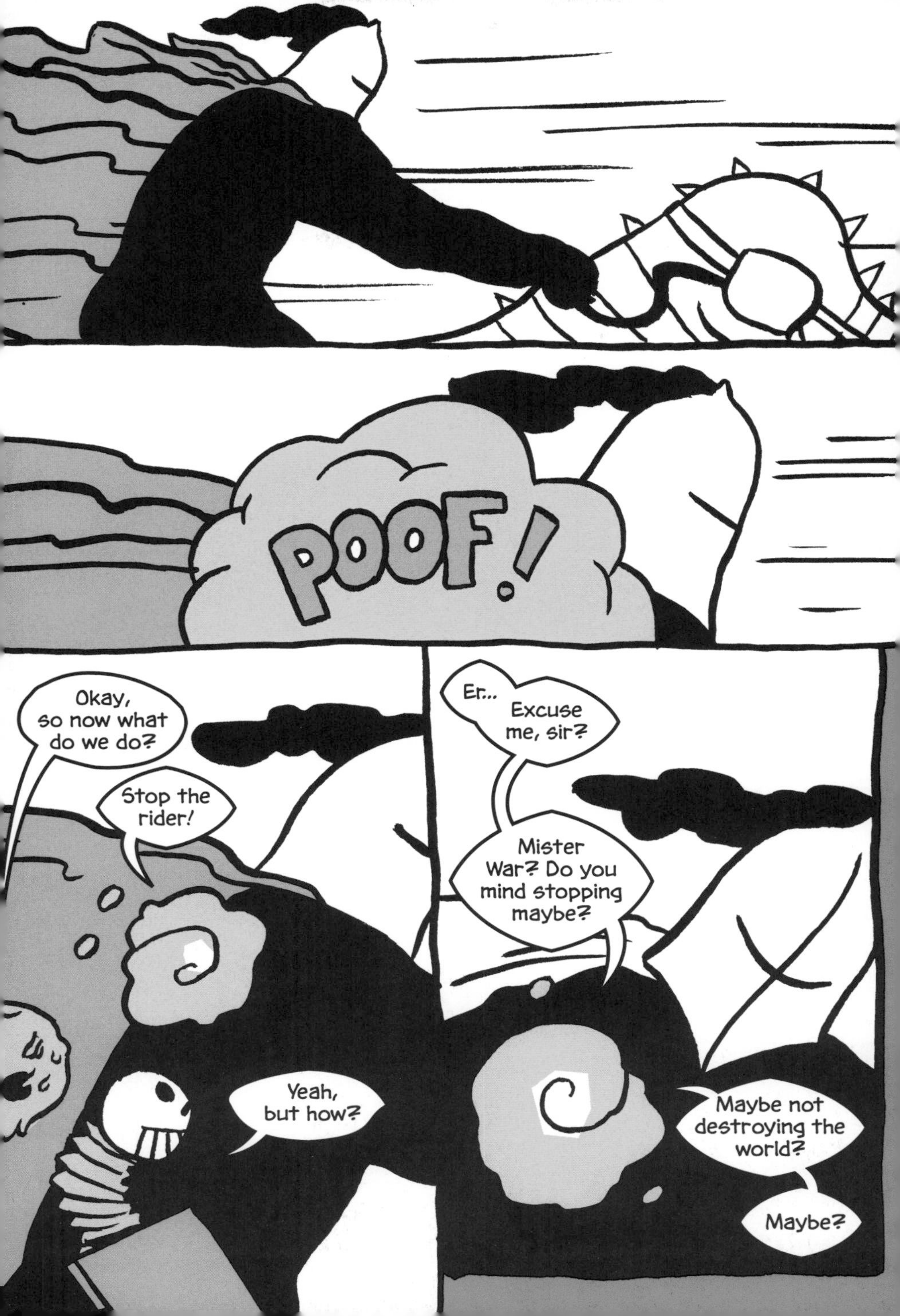
POOF!
Okay, so now what do we do?
Stop the rider!
Yeah, but how?
Er... Excuse me, sir?
Mister War? Do you mind stopping maybe?
Maybe not destroying the world?
Maybe?

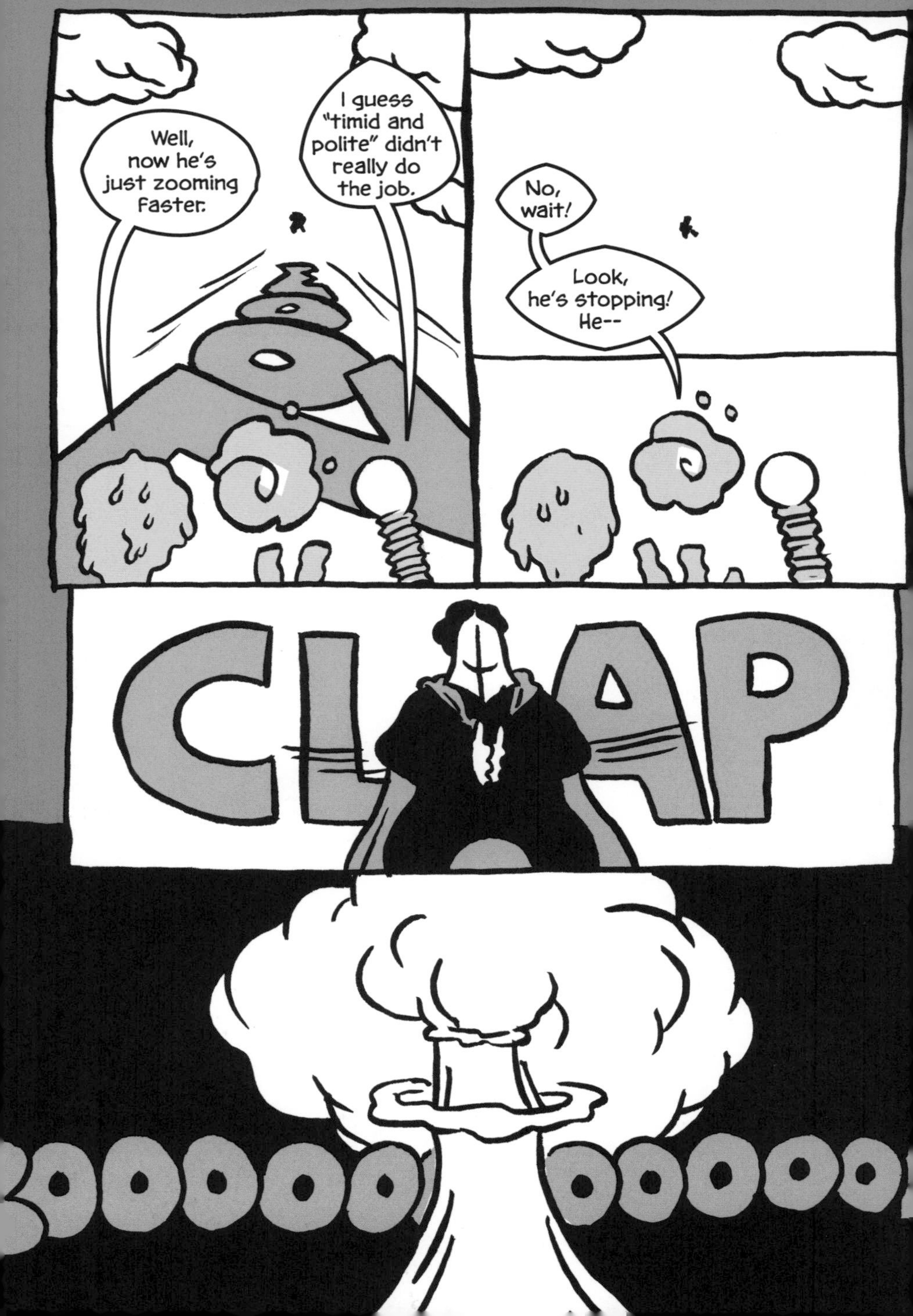
Well, now he's just zooming faster.
I guess "timid and polite" didn't really do the job.
No, wait!
Look, he's stopping! He--
CLAP
BOOOOOOOOOOOOO

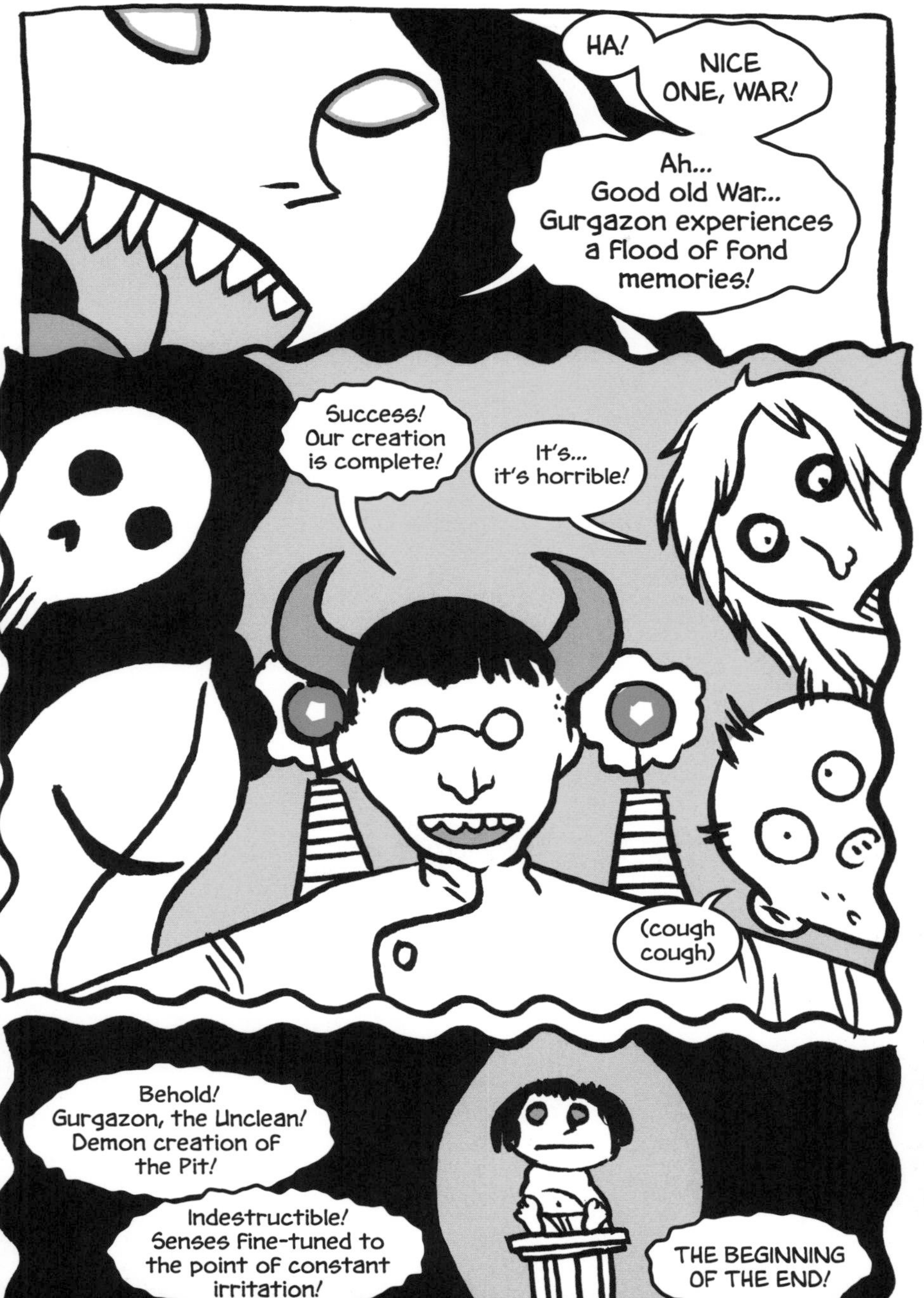
HA!
NICE ONE, WAR!
Ah... Good old War... Gurgazon experiences a flood of fond memories!
Success! Our creation is complete!
It's... it's horrible!
(cough cough)
Behold! Gurgazon, the Unclean! Demon creation of the Pit!
Indestructible! Senses fine-tuned to the point of constant irritation!
THE BEGINNING OF THE END!

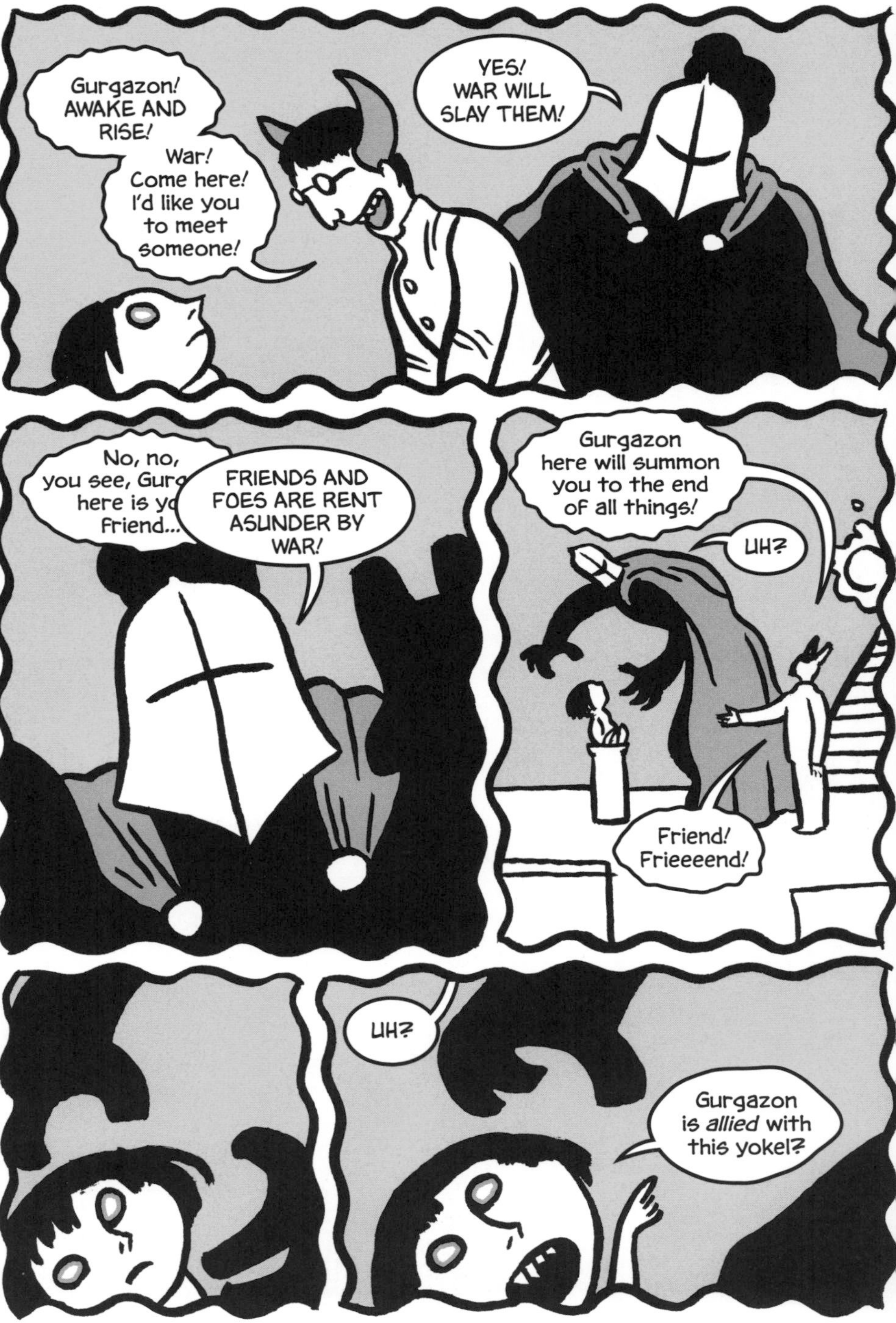
Gurgazon! AWAKE AND RISE!
War! Come here! I'd like you to meet someone!
YES! WAR WILL SLAY THEM!
No, no, you see, Gurg here is yo friend...
FRIENDS AND FOES ARE RENT ASUNDER BY WAR!
Gurgazon here will summon you to the end of all things!
UH?
Friend! Frieeeend!
UH?
Gurgazon is *allied* with this yokel?

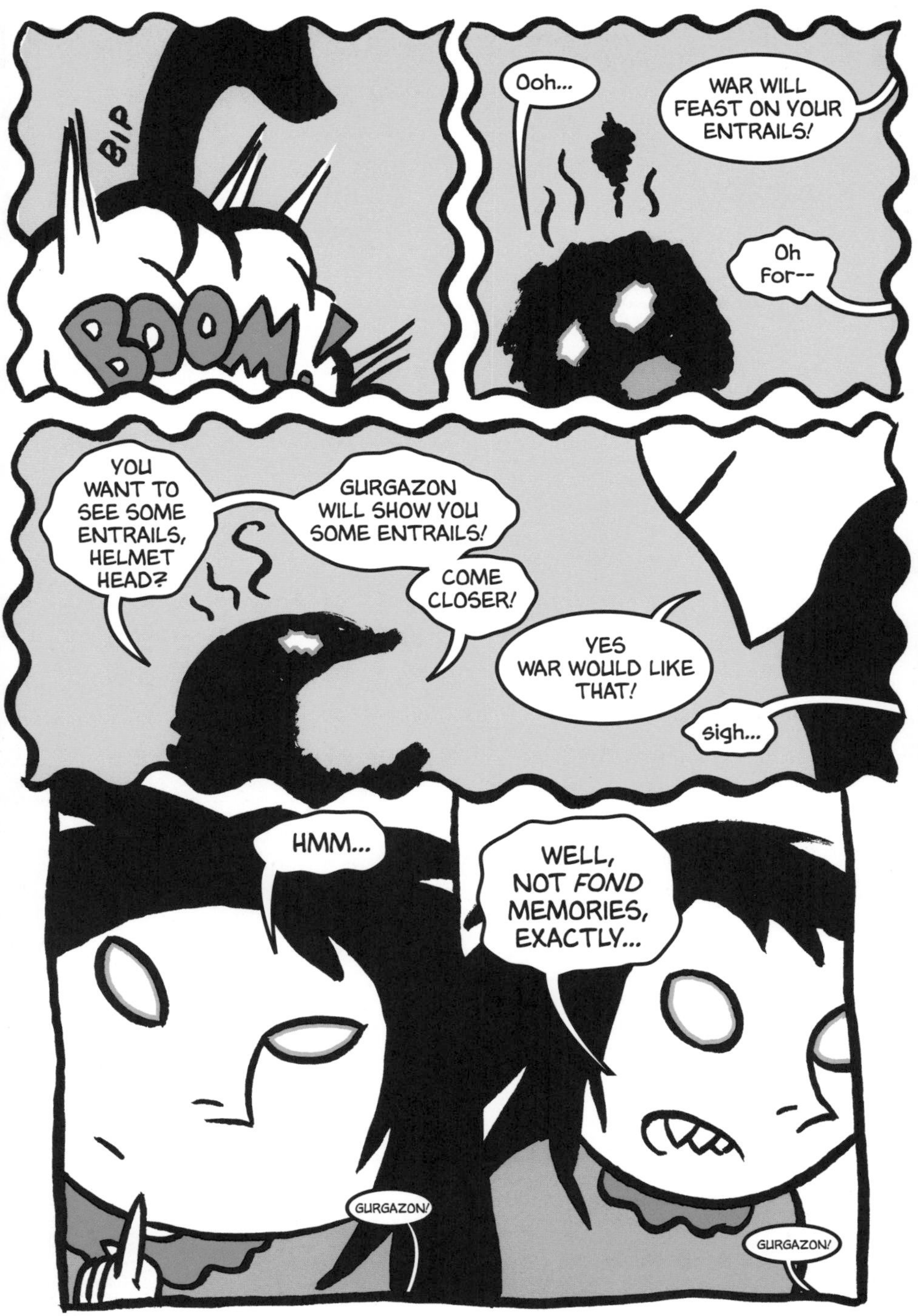
BIP
BOOM!
Ooh...
WAR WILL FEAST ON YOUR ENTRAILS!
Oh for--
YOU WANT TO SEE SOME ENTRAILS, HELMET HEAD?
GURGAZON WILL SHOW YOU SOME ENTRAILS!
COME CLOSER!
YES WAR WOULD LIKE THAT!
sigh...
HMM...
GURGAZON!
WELL, NOT *FOND* MEMORIES, EXACTLY...
GURGAZON!

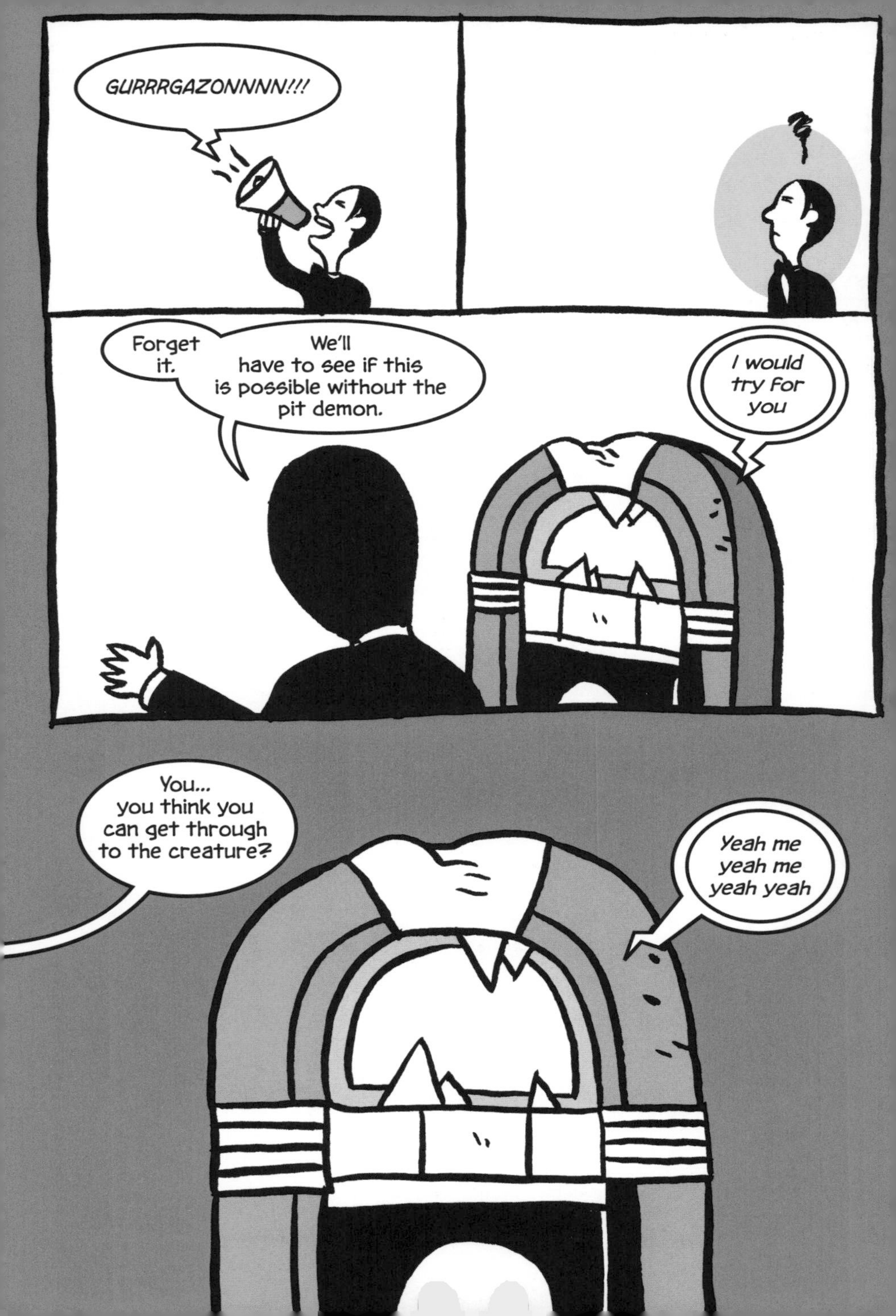
GURRRGAZONNNN!!!
Forget it.
We'll have to see if this is possible without the pit demon.
I would try for you
You... you think you can get through to the creature?
Yeah me yeah me yeah yeah

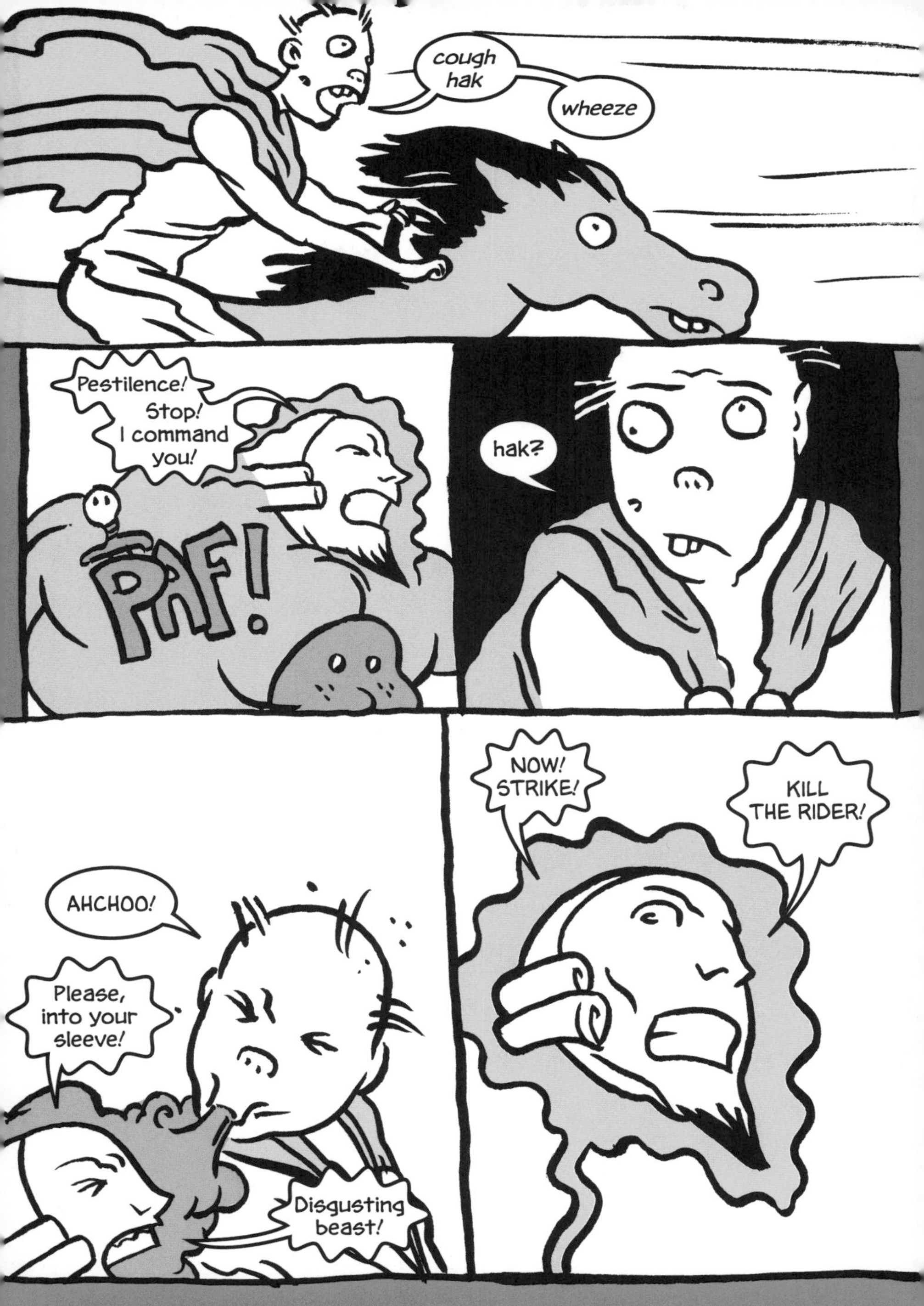

cough hak
wheeze
Pestilence!
Stop! I command you!
PAF!
hak?
AHCHOO!
Please, into your sleeve!
Disgusting beast!
NOW! STRIKE!
KILL THE RIDER!

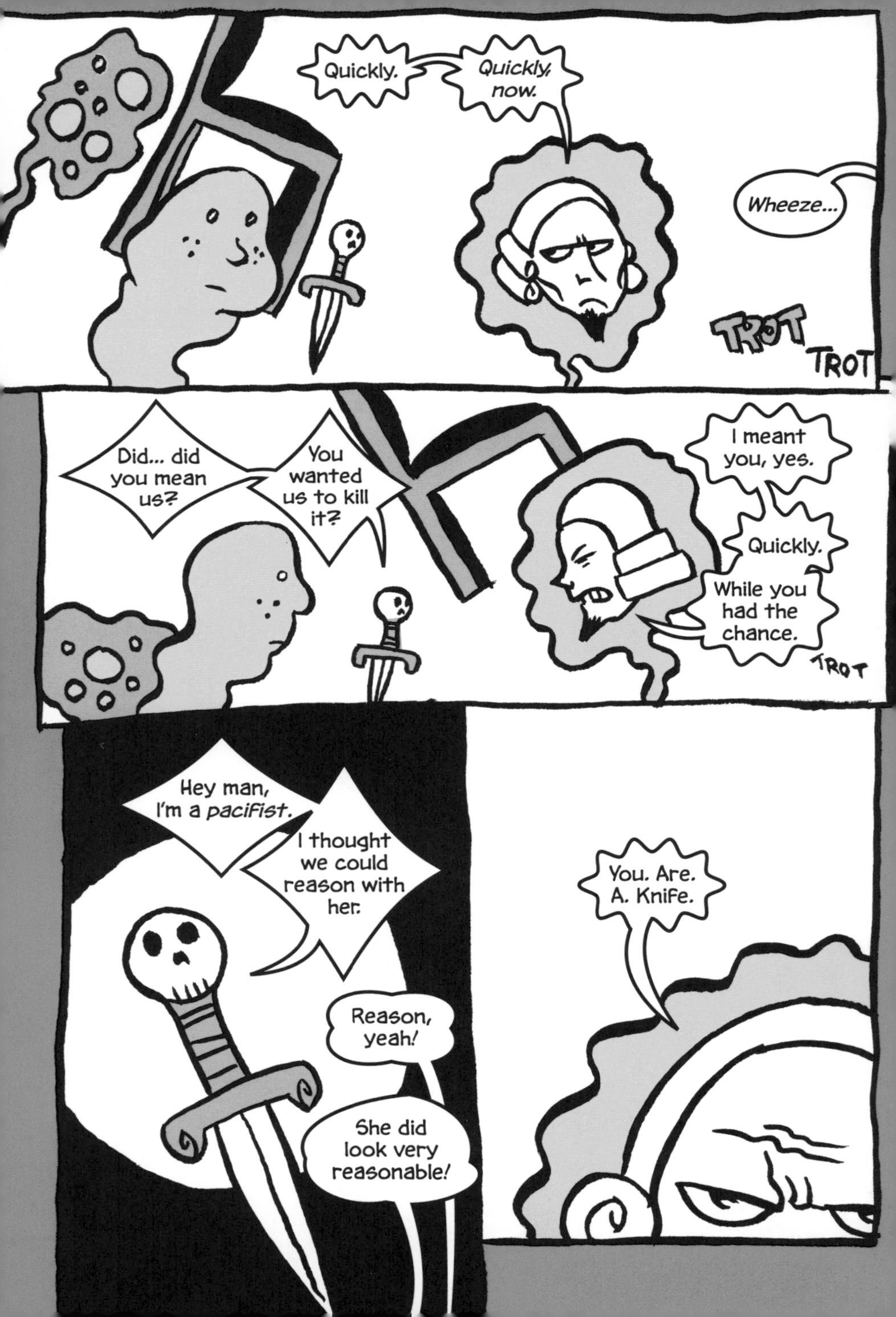

Quickly.
Quickly, now.
Wheeze...
TROT
TROT
Did... did you mean us?
You wanted us to kill it?
I meant you, yes.
Quickly.
While you had the chance.
TROT
Hey man, I'm a *pacifist*.
I thought we could reason with her.
Reason, yeah!
She did look very reasonable!
You. Are. A. Knife.

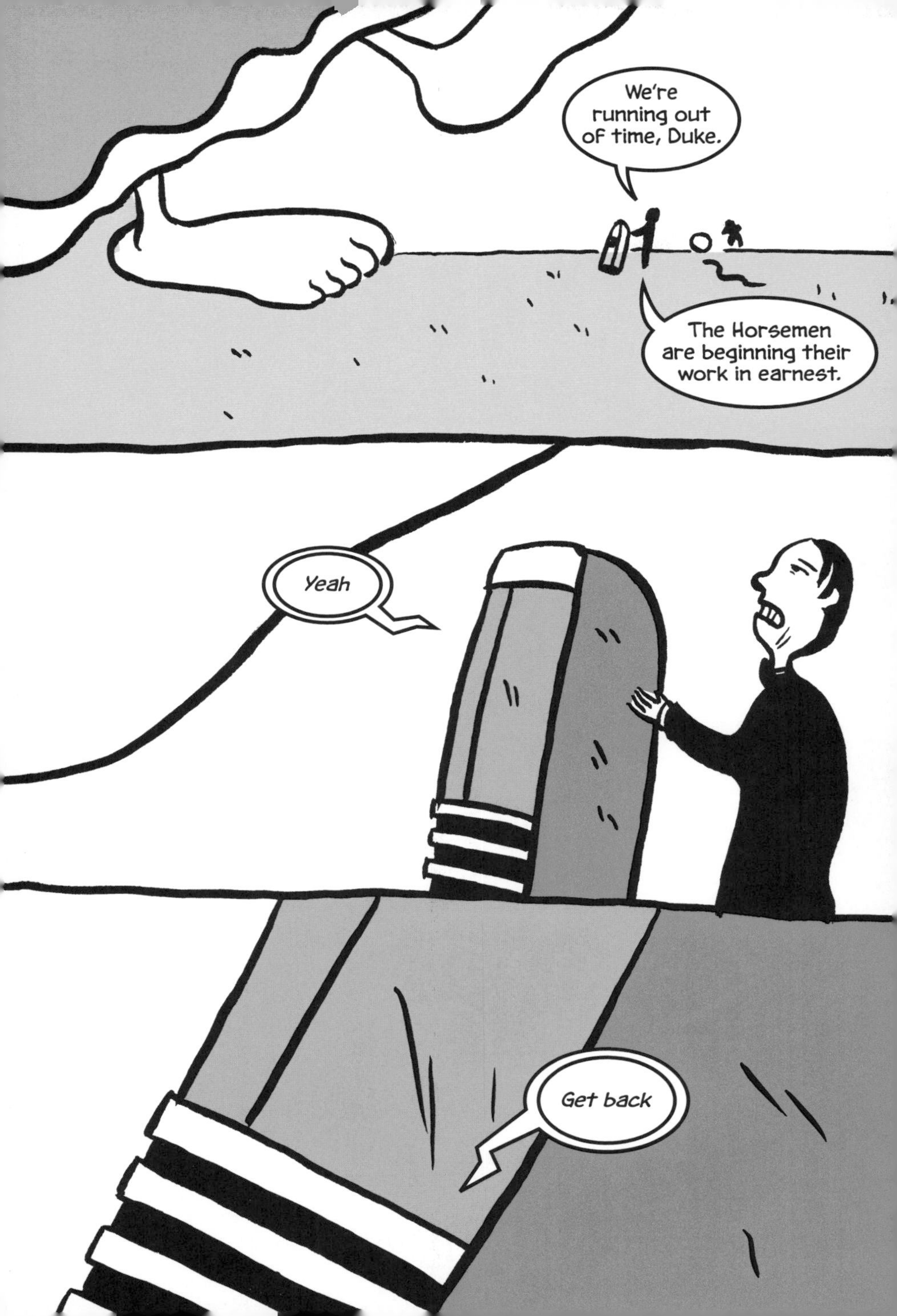
We're running out of time, Duke.
The Horsemen are beginning their work in earnest.
Yeah
Get back

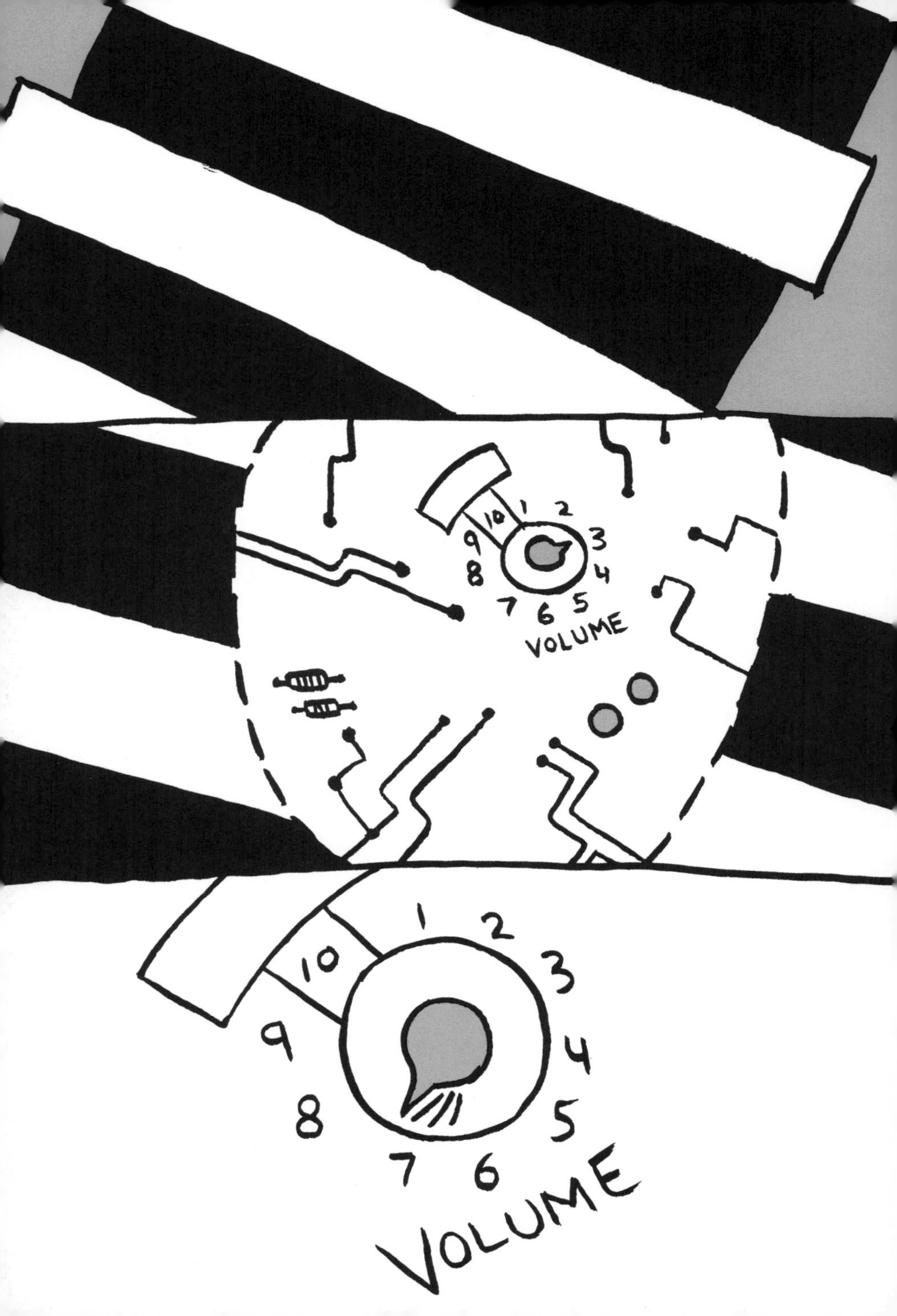
10 1 2 3 4 5 6 7 8 9
VOLUME
10 1 2 3 4 5 6 7 8 9
VOLUME

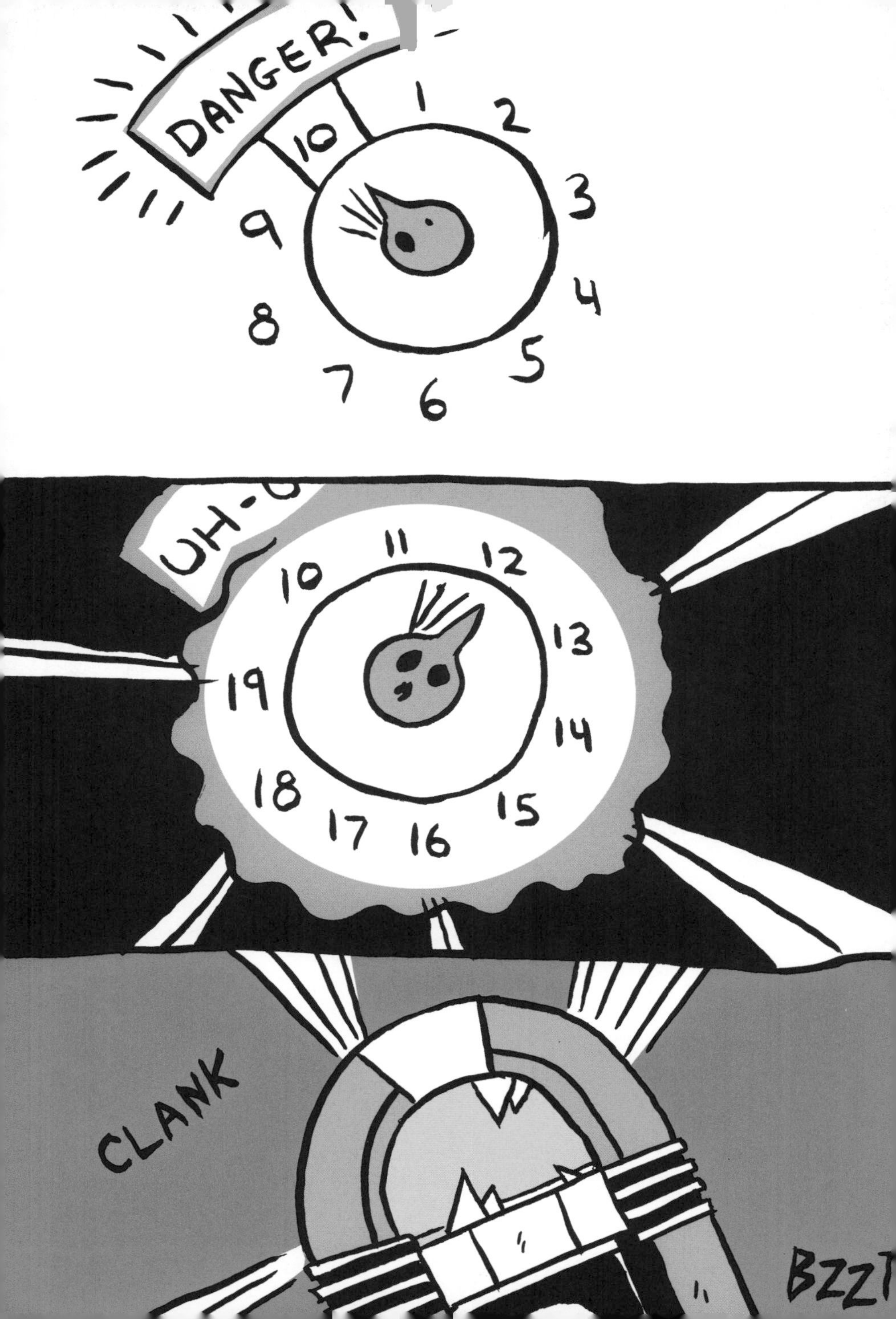
DANGER!
10
1
2
3
4
5
6
7
8
9
UH-O
11
12
13
14
15
16
17
18
19
10
CLANK
BZZT

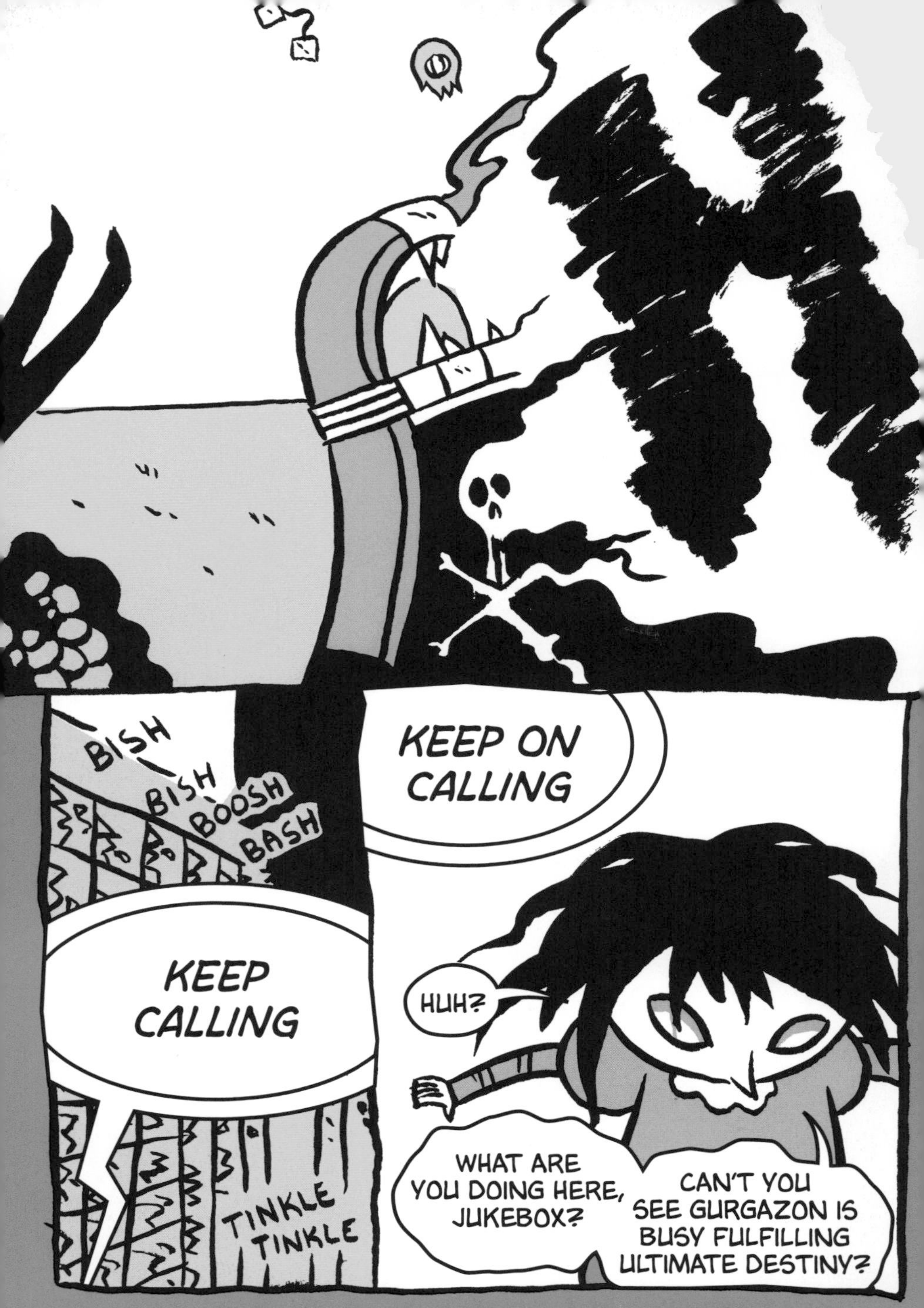
BISH
BISH
BOOSH
BASH
KEEP ON CALLING
KEEP CALLING
TINKLE TINKLE
HUH?
WHAT ARE YOU DOING HERE, JUKEBOX?
CAN'T YOU SEE GURGAZON IS BUSY FULFILLING ULTIMATE DESTINY?

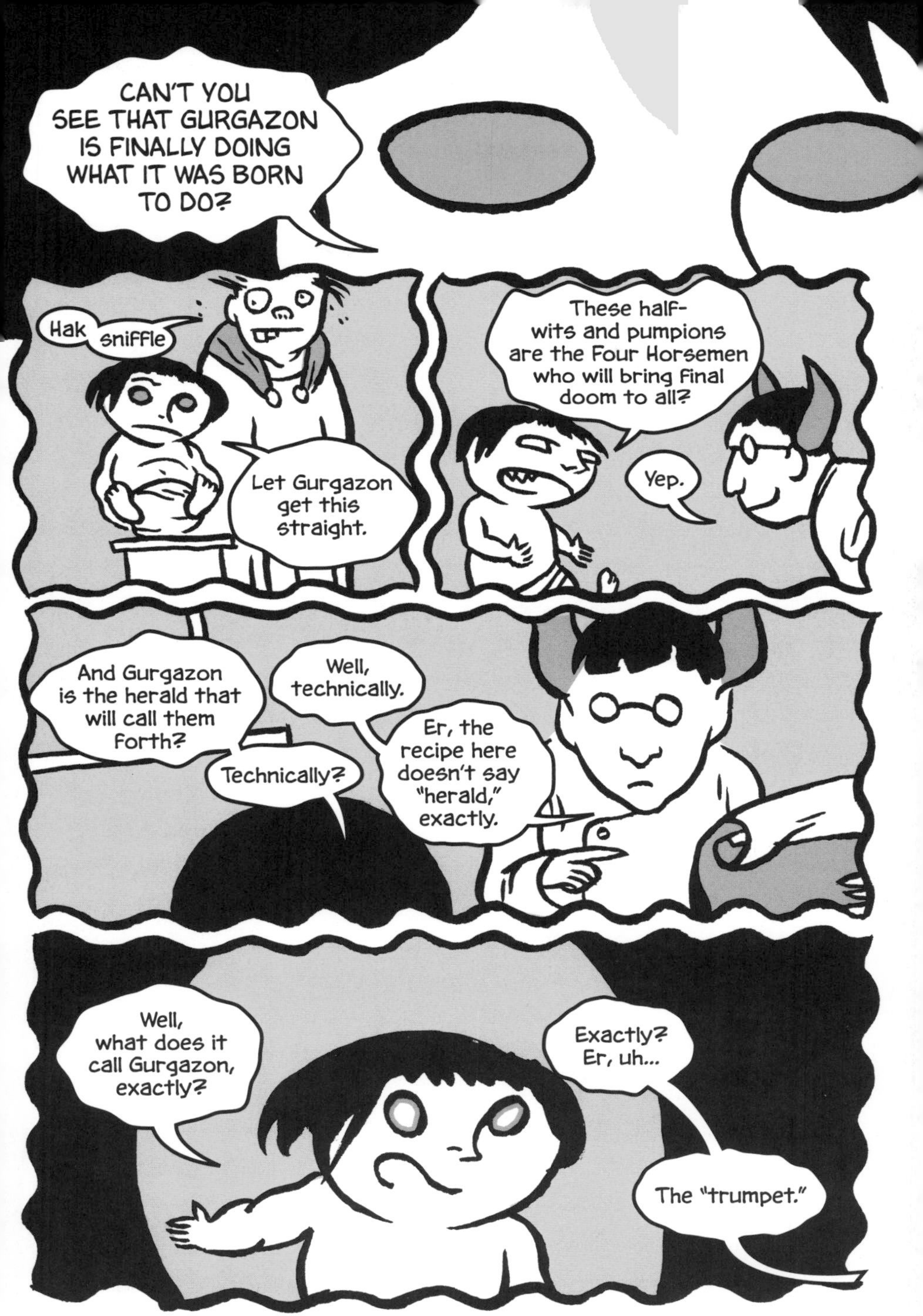
CAN'T YOU SEE THAT GURGAZON IS FINALLY DOING WHAT IT WAS BORN TO DO?
Hak
sniffle
Let Gurgazon get this straight.
These half-wits and pumpions are the Four Horsemen who will bring final doom to all?
Yep.
And Gurgazon is the herald that will call them forth?
Well, technically.
Technically?
Er, the recipe here doesn't say "herald," exactly.
Well, what does it call Gurgazon, exactly?
Exactly? Er, uh...
The "trumpet."

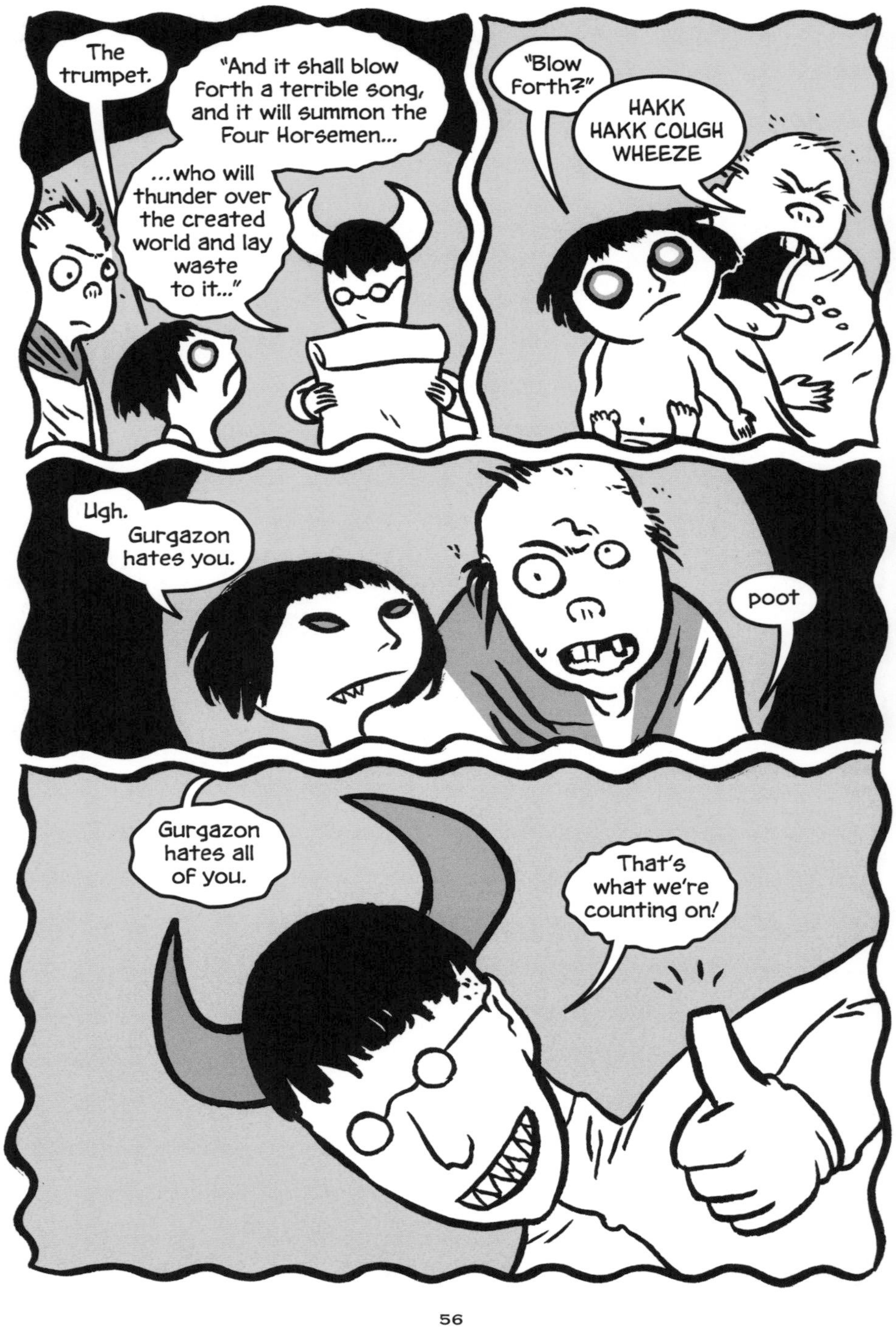
The trumpet.
"And it shall blow forth a terrible song, and it will summon the Four Horsemen...
...who will thunder over the created world and lay waste to it..."
"Blow forth?"
HAKK HAKK COUGH WHEEZE
Ugh. Gurgazon hates you.
poot
Gurgazon hates all of you.
That's what we're counting on!

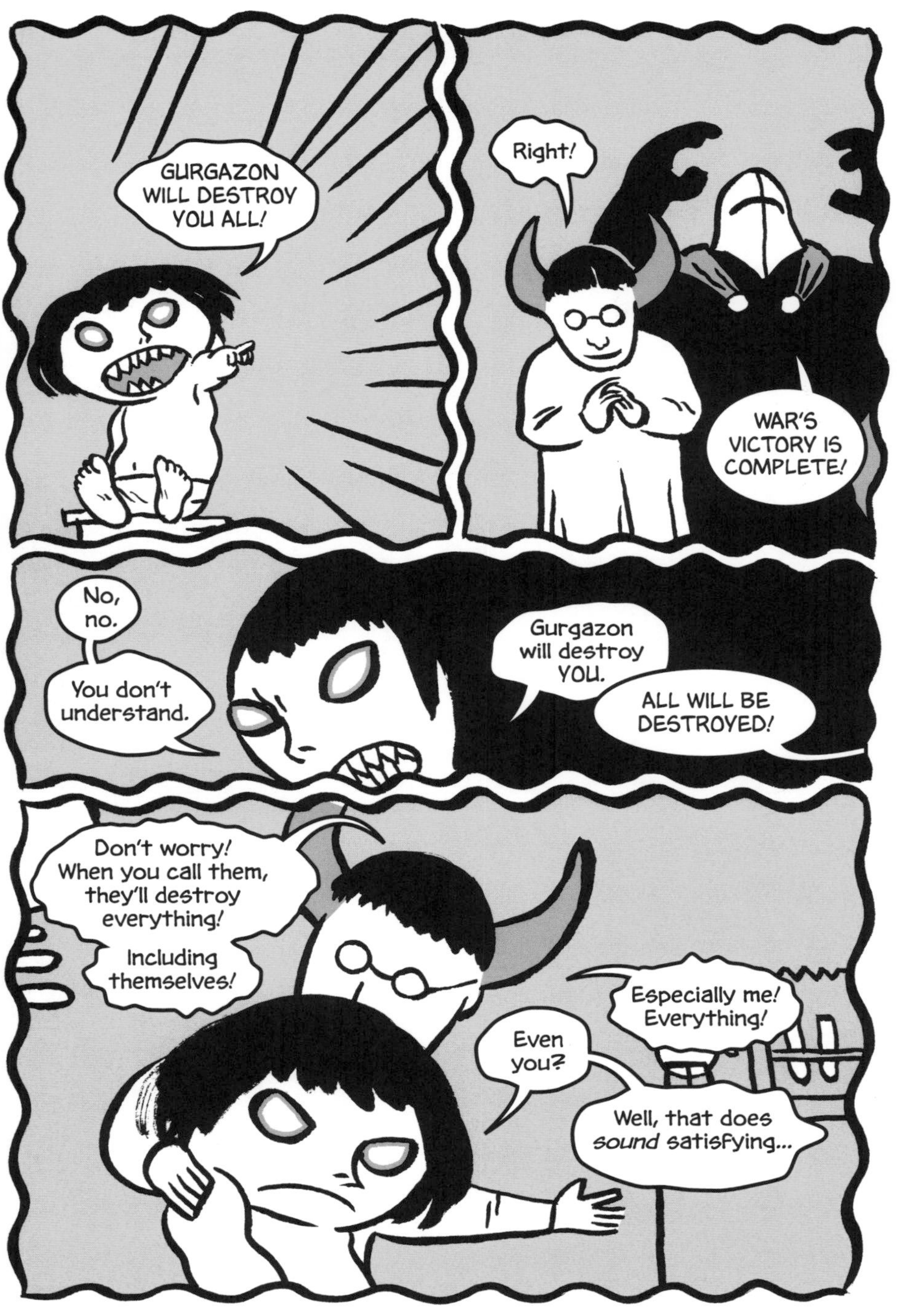
GURGAZON WILL DESTROY YOU ALL!
Right!
WAR'S VICTORY IS COMPLETE!
No, no.
You don't understand.
Gurgazon will destroy YOU.
ALL WILL BE DESTROYED!
Don't worry! When you call them, they'll destroy everything!
Including themselves!
Even you?
Especially me! Everything!
Well, that does *sound* satisfying...

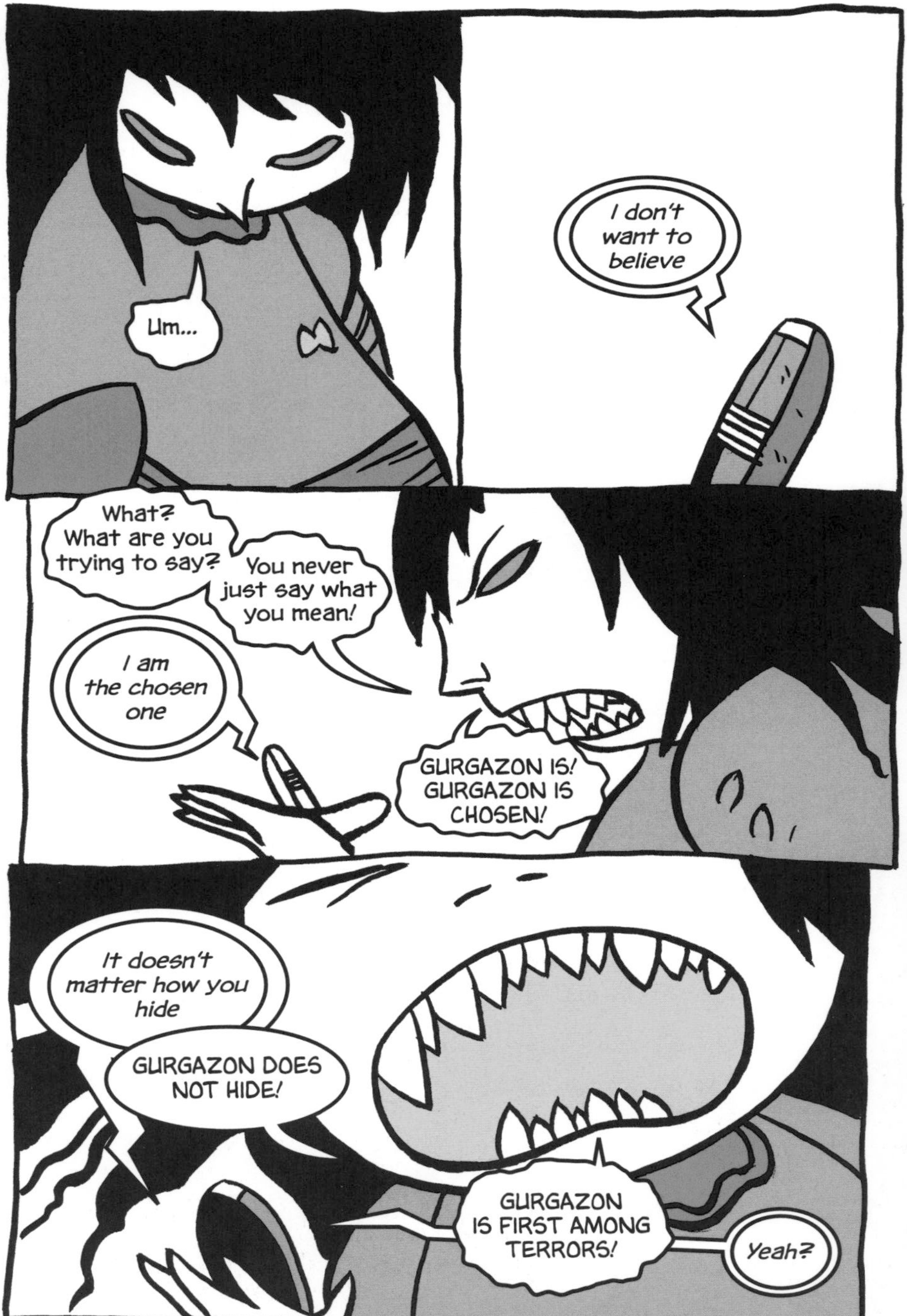

Um...
I don't want to believe
What? What are you trying to say?
You never just say what you mean!
I am the chosen one
GURGAZON IS! GURGAZON IS CHOSEN!
It doesn't matter how you hide
GURGAZON DOES NOT HIDE!
GURGAZON IS FIRST AMONG TERRORS!
Yeah?

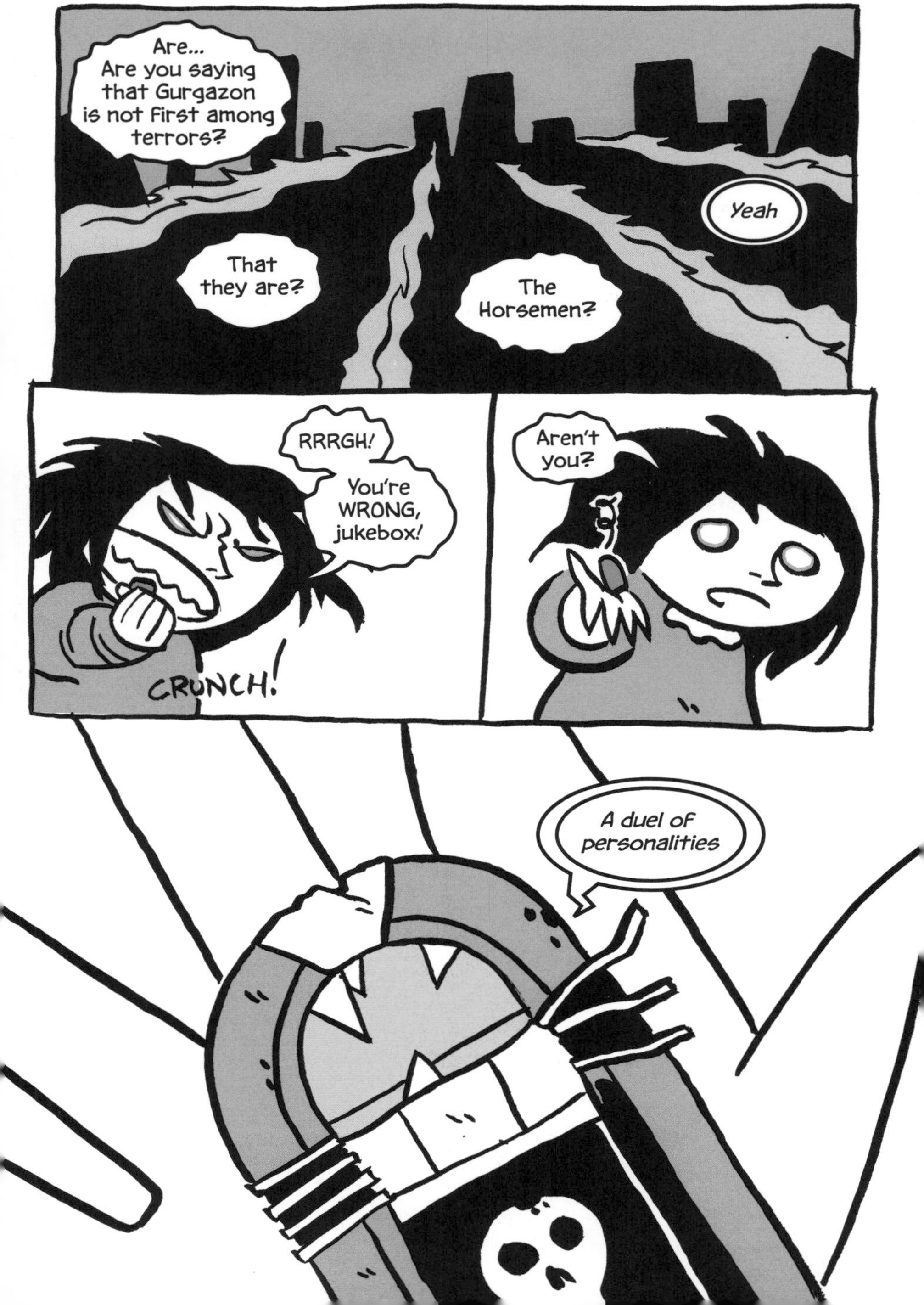
Are... Are you saying that Gurgazon is not first among terrors?
Yeah
That they are?
The Horsemen?
RRRGH!
You're WRONG, jukebox!
CRUNCH!
Aren't you?
A duel of personalities

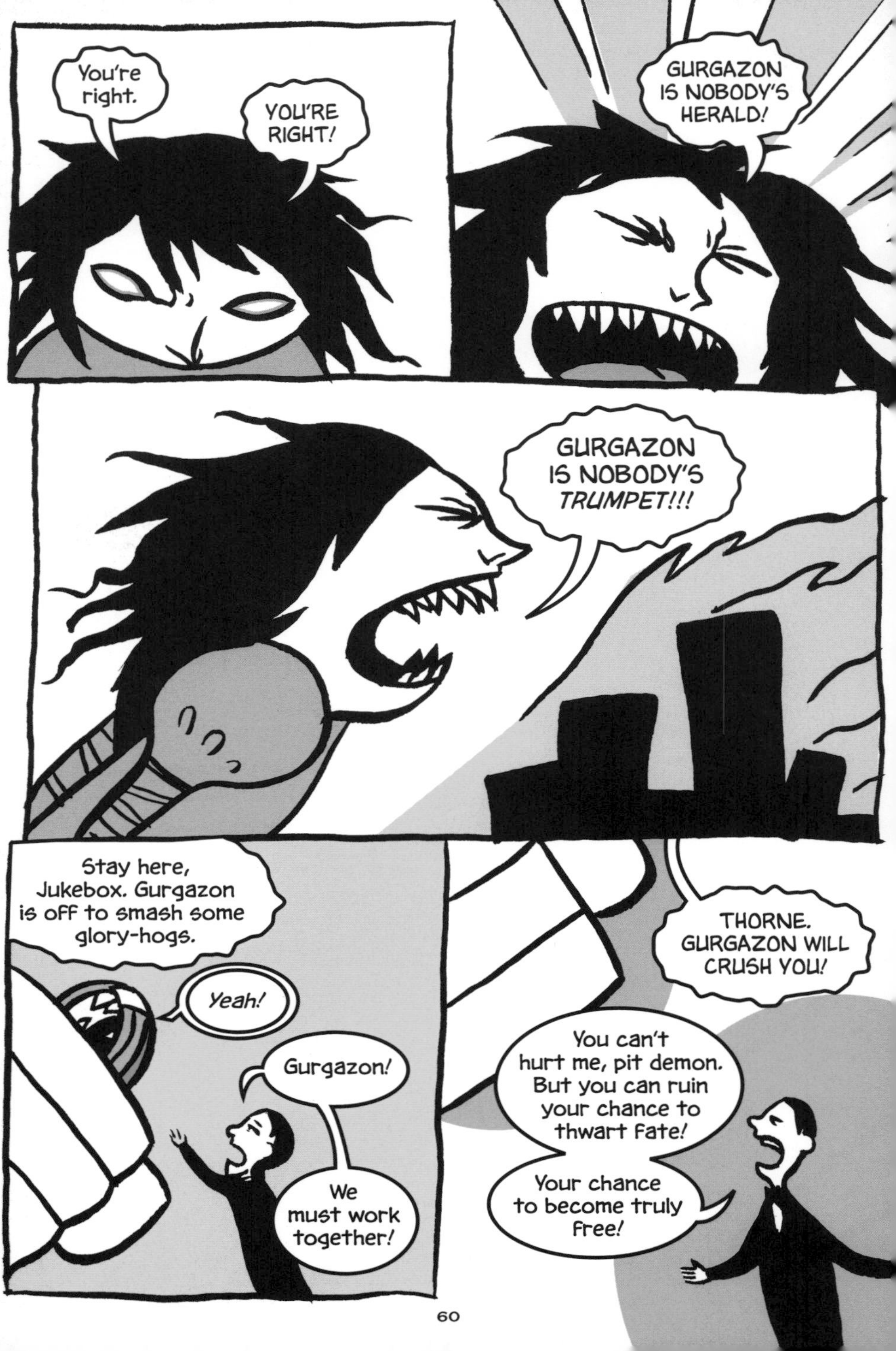

You're right.
YOU'RE RIGHT!
GURGAZON IS NOBODY'S HERALD!
GURGAZON IS NOBODY'S *TRUMPET!!!*
Stay here, Jukebox. Gurgazon is off to smash some glory-hogs.
Yeah!
Gurgazon!
We must work together!
THORNE. GURGAZON WILL CRUSH YOU!
You can't hurt me, pit demon. But you can ruin your chance to thwart fate!
Your chance to become truly free!

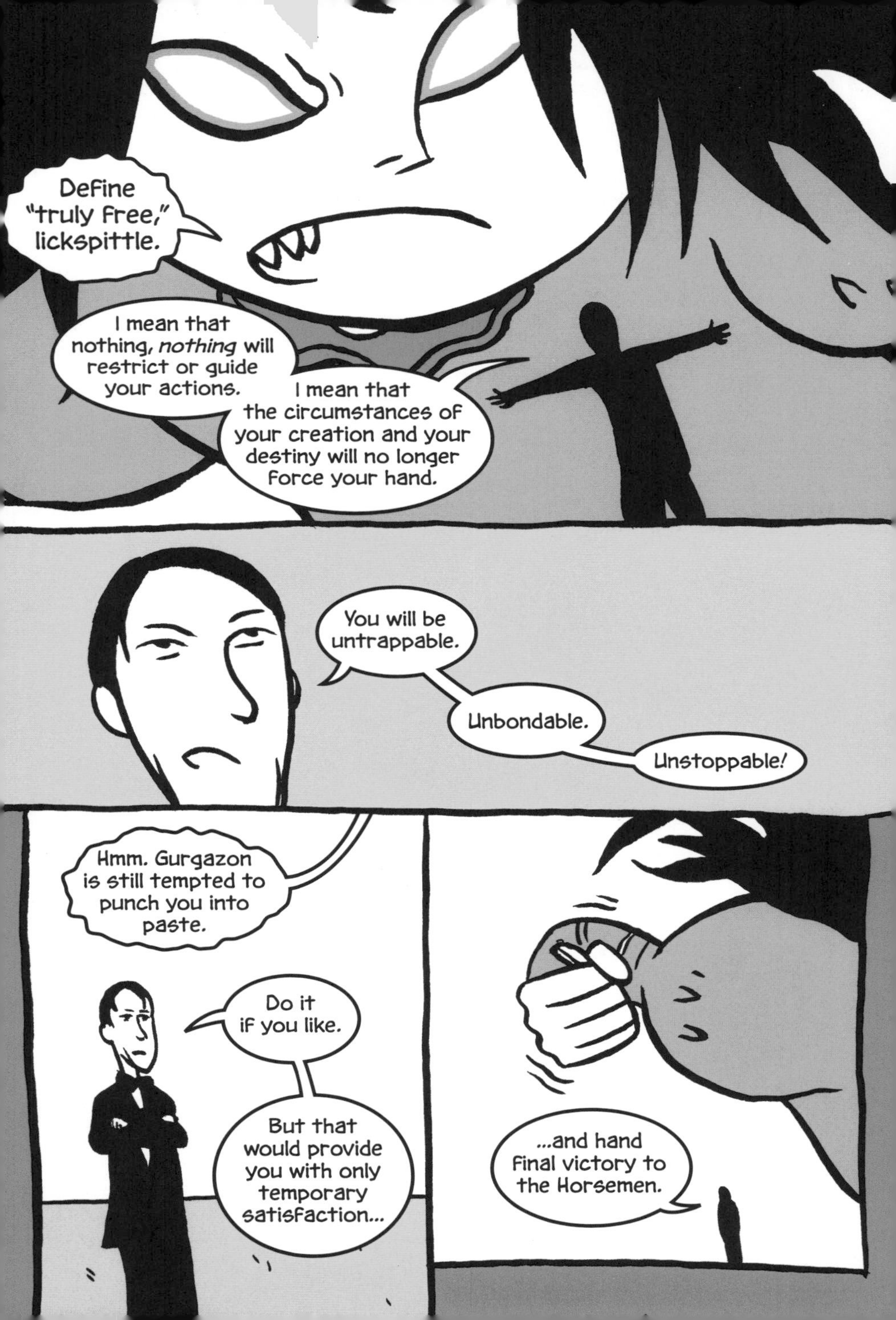
Define "truly free," lickspittle.
I mean that nothing, *nothing* will restrict or guide your actions.
I mean that the circumstances of your creation and your destiny will no longer force your hand.
You will be untrappable.
Unbondable.
Unstoppable!
Hmm. Gurgazon is still tempted to punch you into paste.
Do it if you like.
But that would provide you with only temporary satisfaction...
...and hand final victory to the Horsemen.

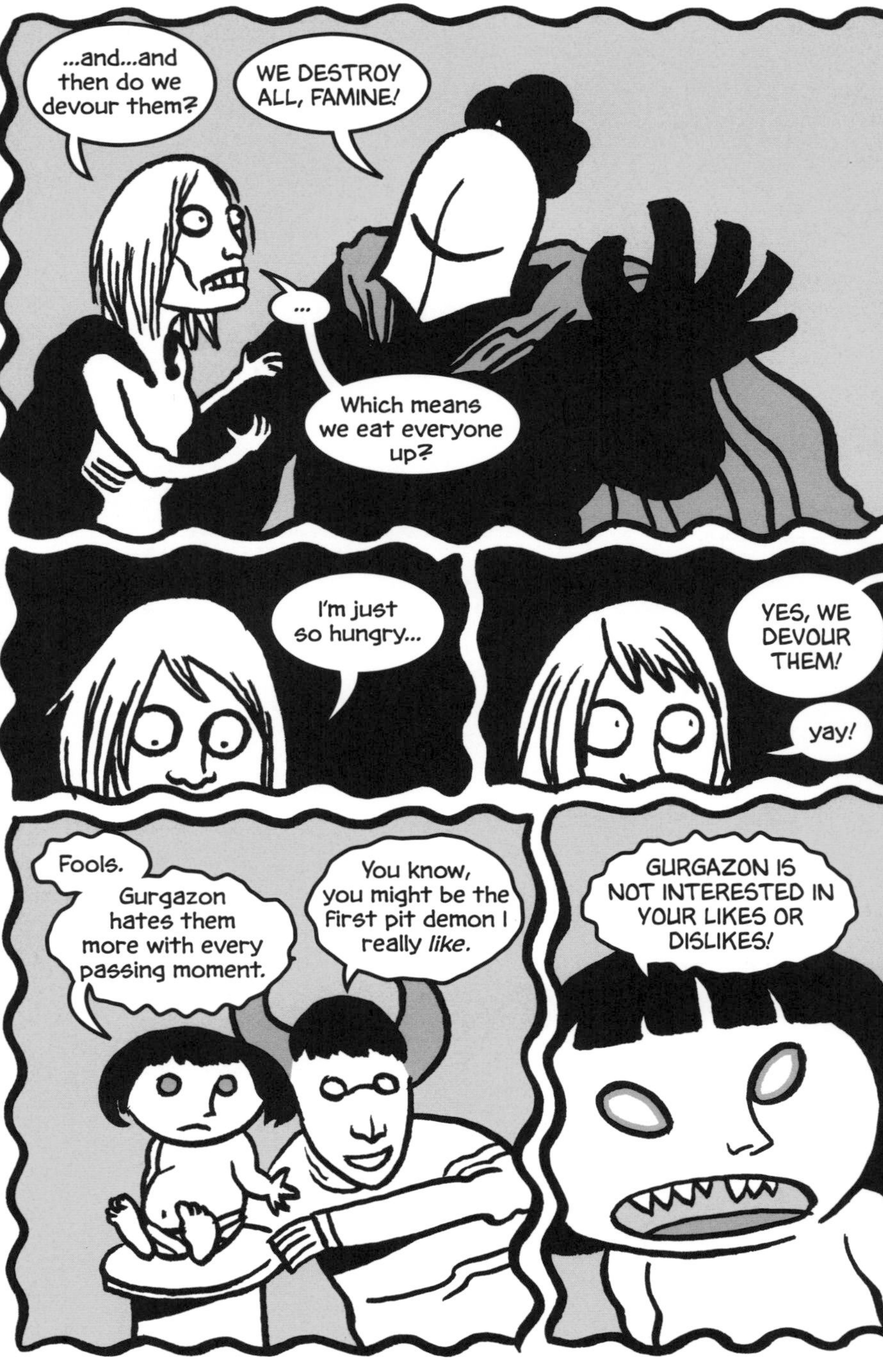
...and...and then do we devour them?
WE DESTROY ALL, FAMINE!
...
Which means we eat everyone up?
I'm just so hungry...
YES, WE DEVOUR THEM!
yay!
Fools.
Gurgazon hates them more with every passing moment.
You know, you might be the first pit demon I really *like.*
GURGAZON IS NOT INTERESTED IN YOUR LIKES OR DISLIKES!

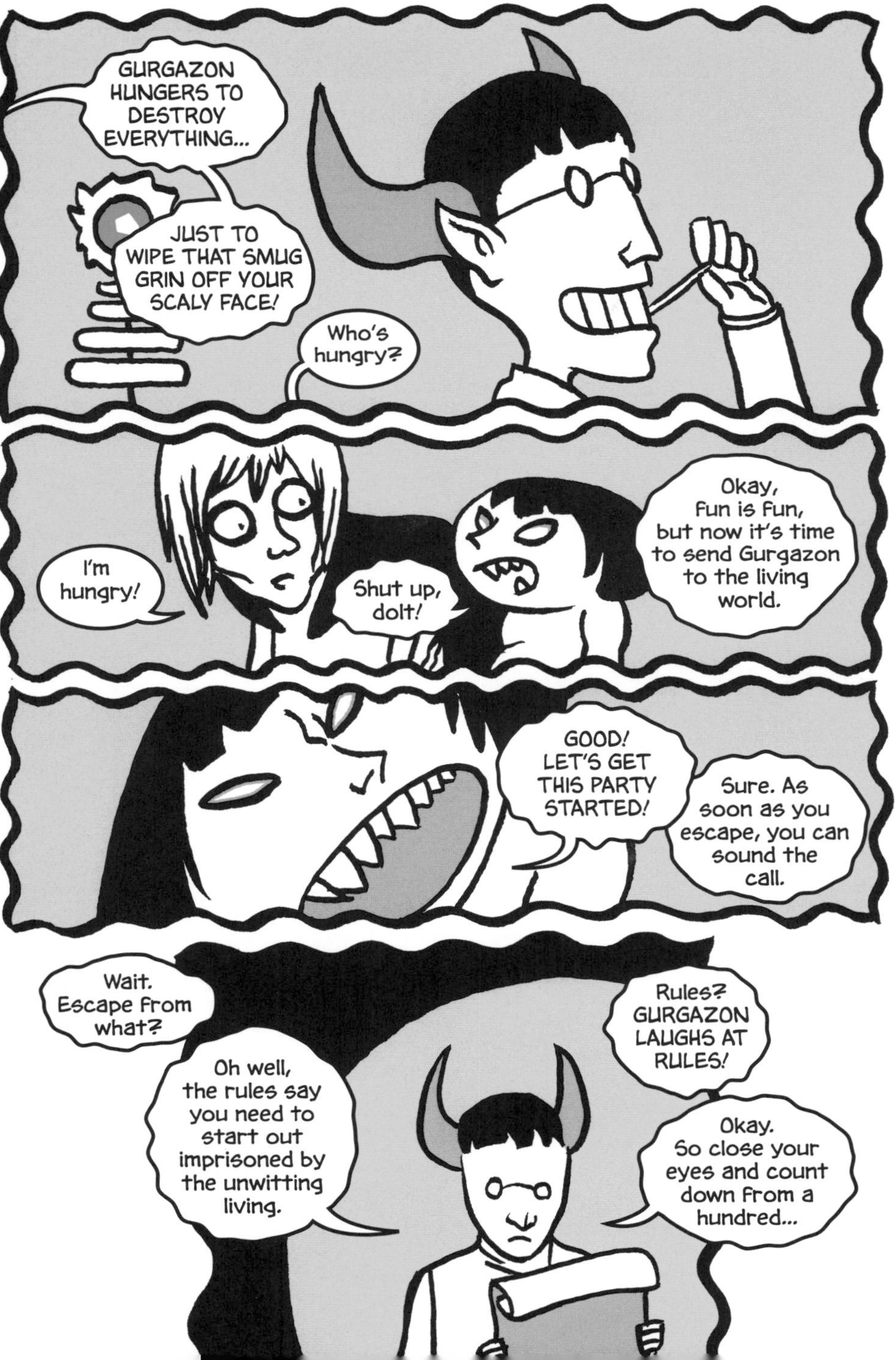
GURGAZON HUNGERS TO DESTROY EVERYTHING...
JUST TO WIPE THAT SMUG GRIN OFF YOUR SCALY FACE!
Who's hungry?
I'm hungry!
Shut up, dolt!
Okay, fun is fun, but now it's time to send Gurgazon to the living world.
GOOD! LET'S GET THIS PARTY STARTED!
Sure. As soon as you escape, you can sound the call.
Wait. Escape from what?
Oh well, the rules say you need to start out imprisoned by the unwitting living.
Rules? GURGAZON LAUGHS AT RULES!
Okay. So close your eyes and count down from a hundred...

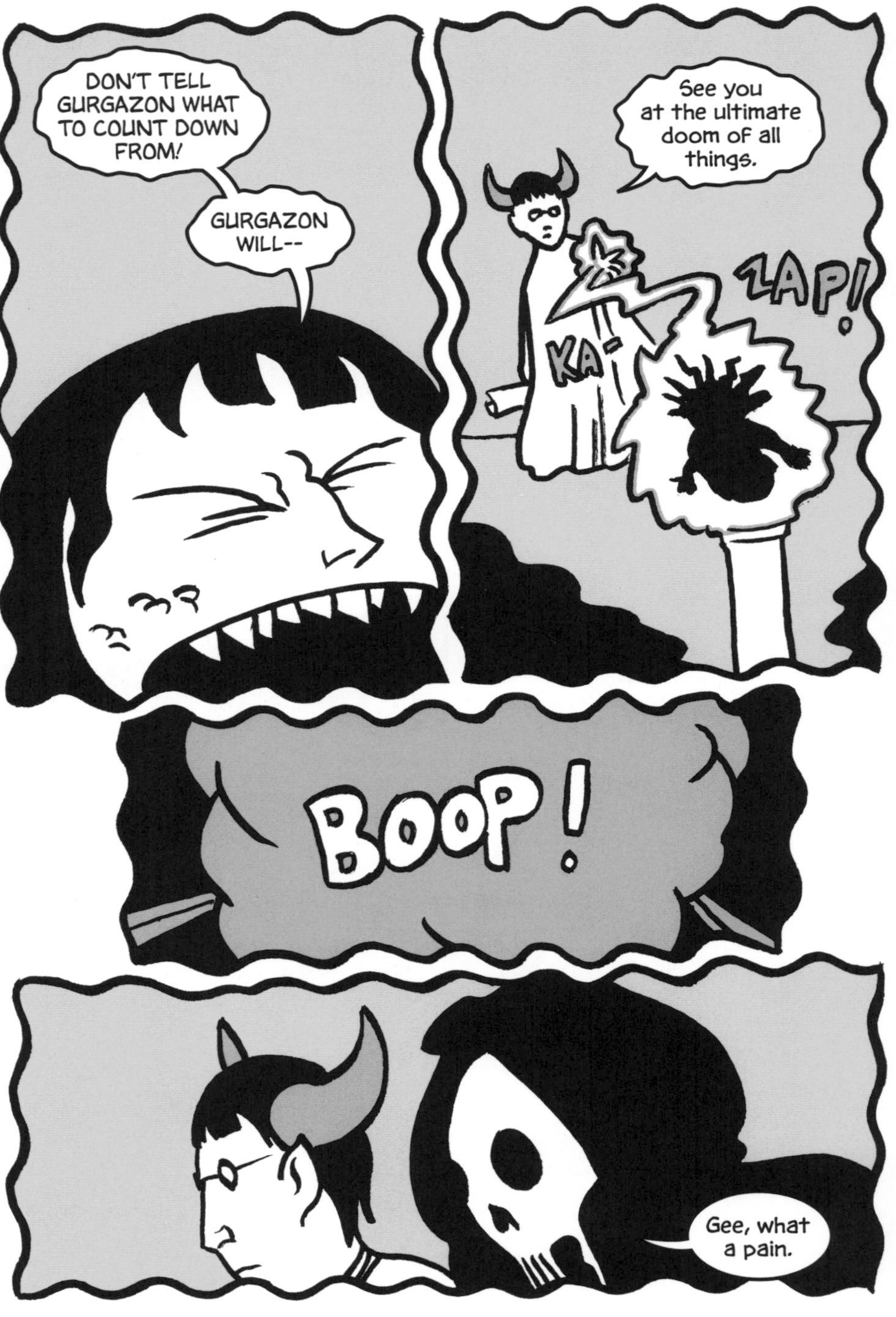
DON'T TELL GURGAZON WHAT TO COUNT DOWN FROM!
GURGAZON WILL--
See you at the ultimate doom of all things.
KA-
ZAP!
BOOP!
Gee, what a pain.

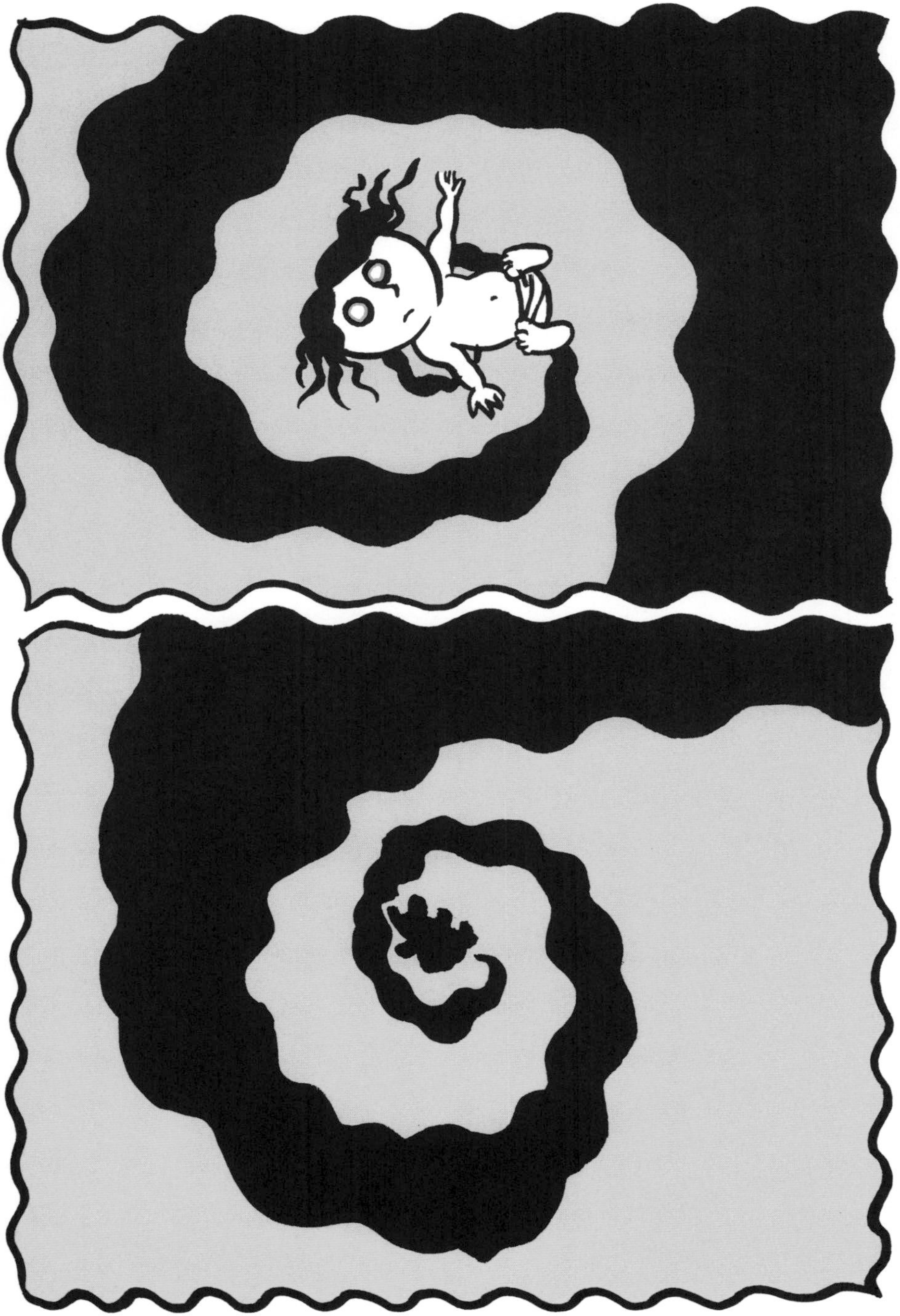

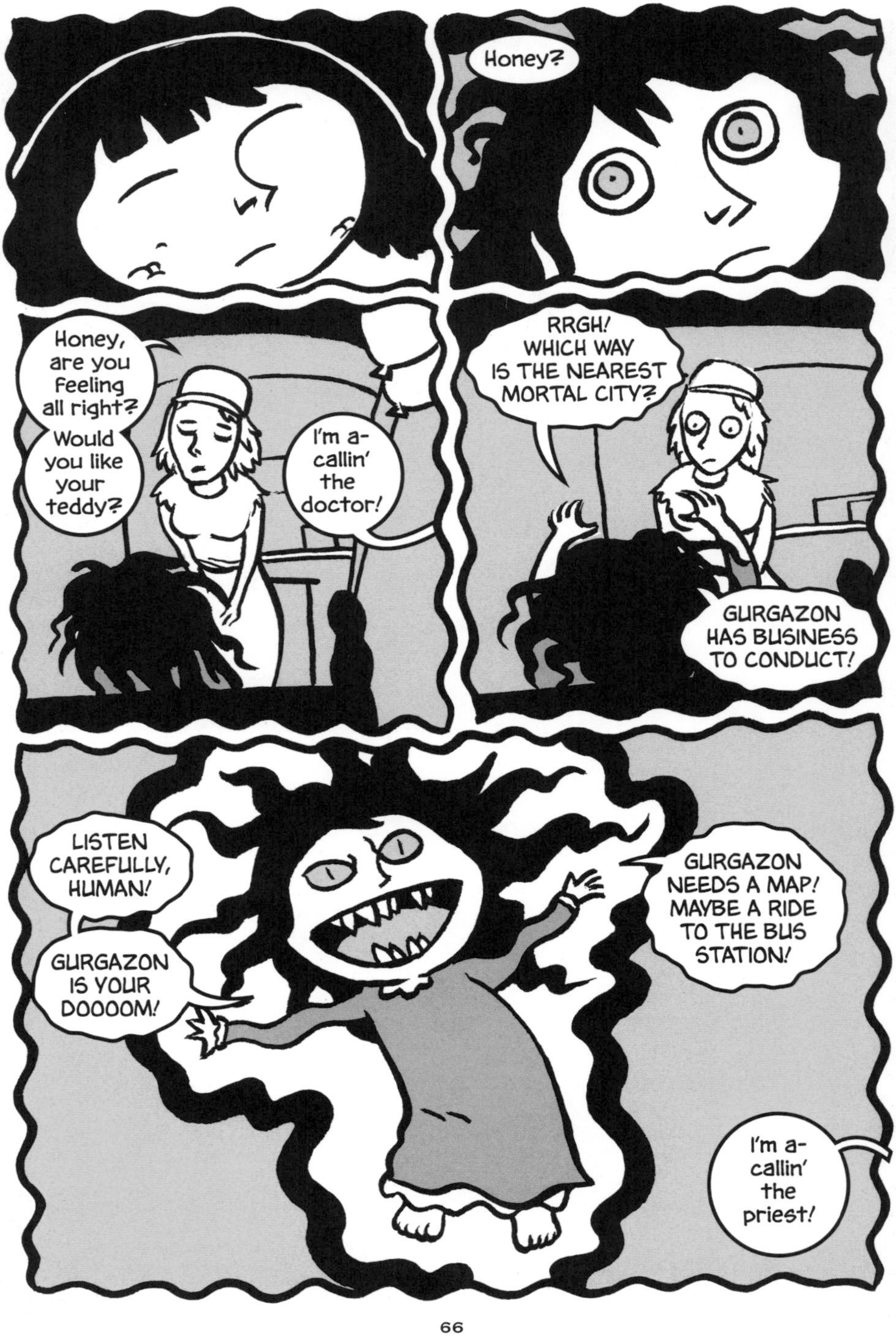

Honey?
Honey, are you feeling all right?
Would you like your teddy?
I'm a-callin' the doctor!
RRGH! WHICH WAY IS THE NEAREST MORTAL CITY?
GURGAZON HAS BUSINESS TO CONDUCT!
LISTEN CAREFULLY, HUMAN!
GURGAZON IS YOUR DOOOOM!
GURGAZON NEEDS A MAP! MAYBE A RIDE TO THE BUS STATION!
I'm a-callin' the priest!

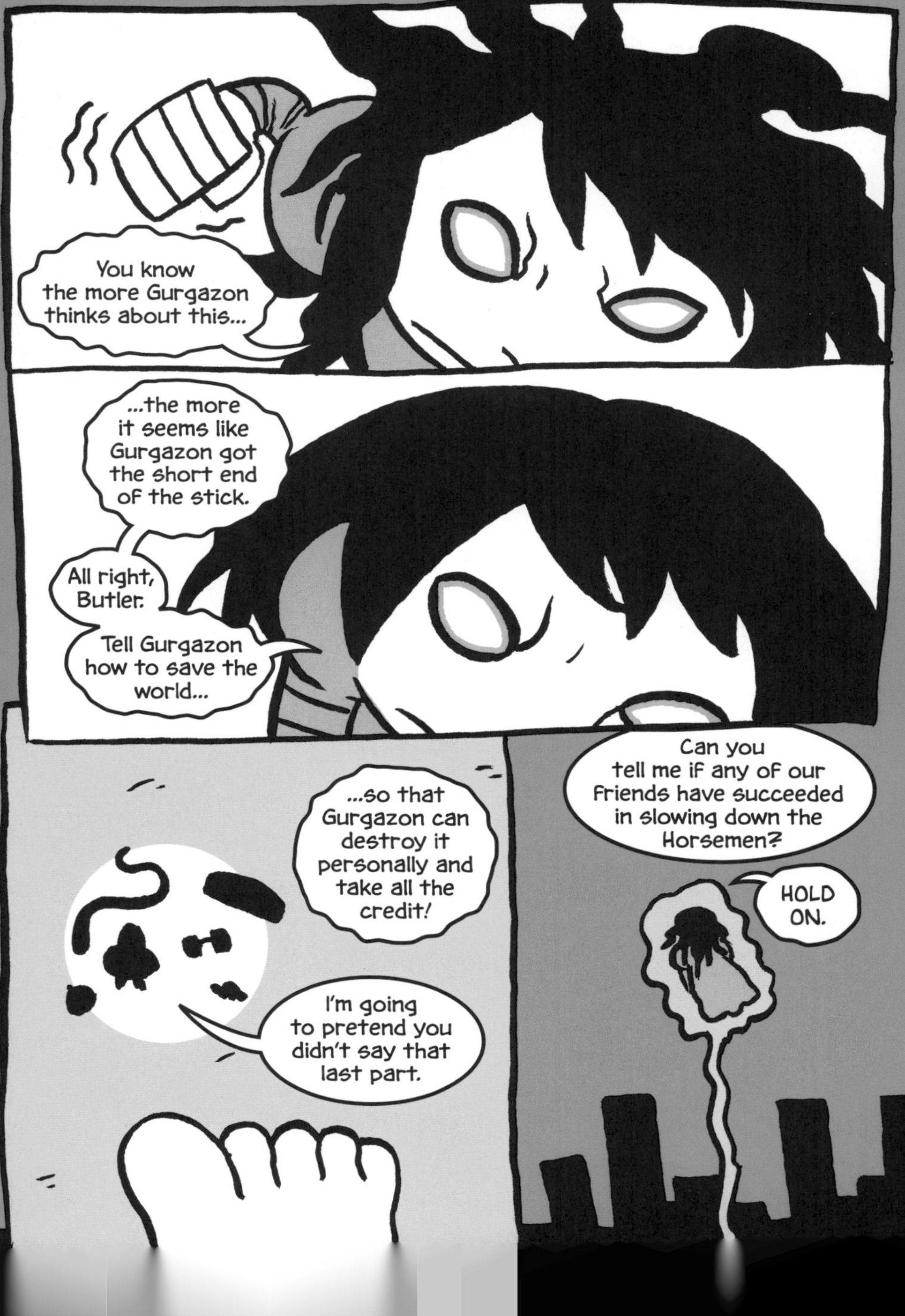
You know the more Gurgazon thinks about this...
...the more it seems like Gurgazon got the short end of the stick.
All right, Butler.
Tell Gurgazon how to save the world...
...so that Gurgazon can destroy it personally and take all the credit!
I'm going to pretend you didn't say that last part.
Can you tell me if any of our friends have succeeded in slowing down the Horsemen?
HOLD ON.

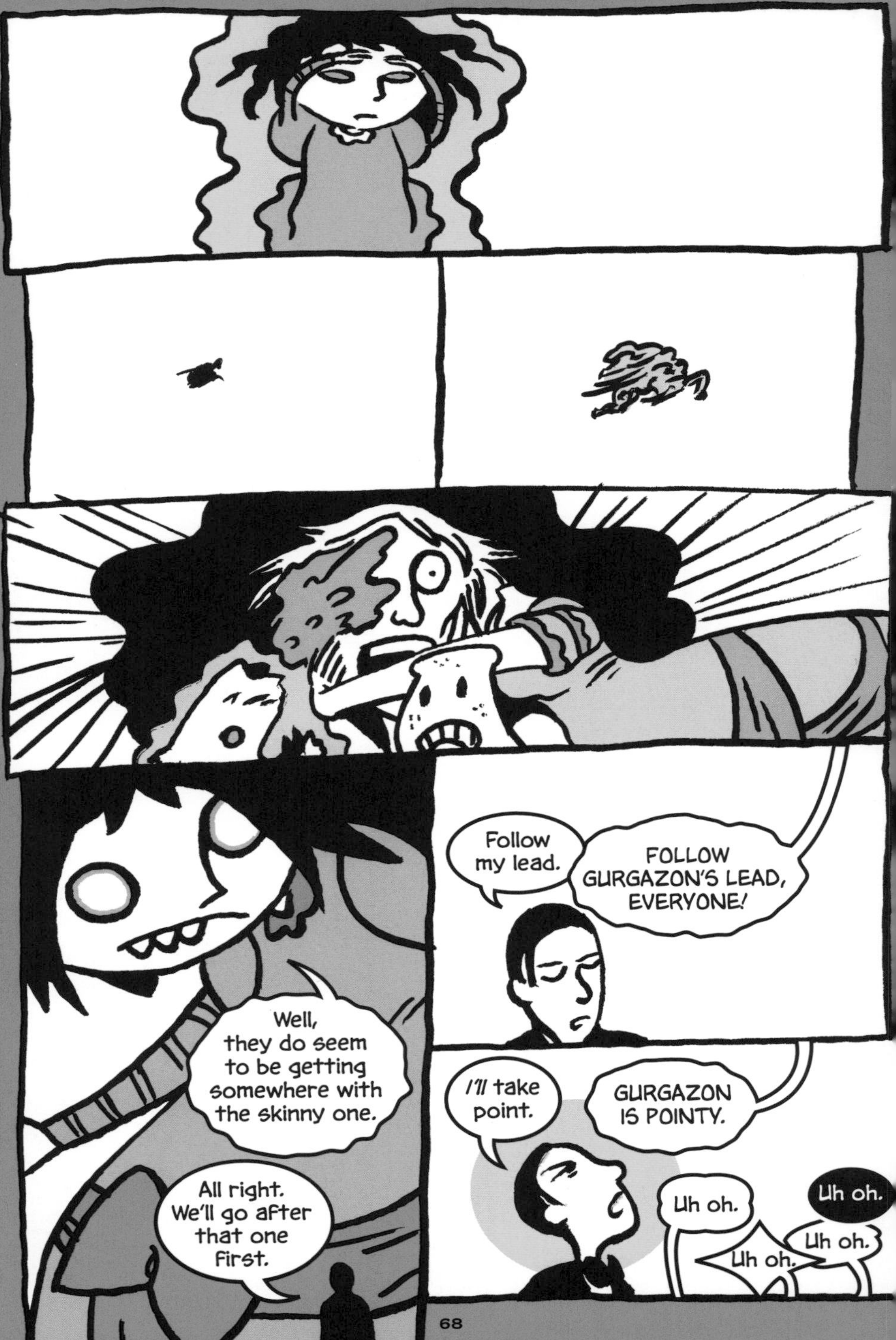
Well, they do seem to be getting somewhere with the skinny one.
All right. We'll go after that one first.
Follow my lead.
FOLLOW GURGAZON'S LEAD, EVERYONE!
I'll take point.
GURGAZON IS POINTY.
Uh oh.
Uh oh.
Uh oh.
Uh oh.

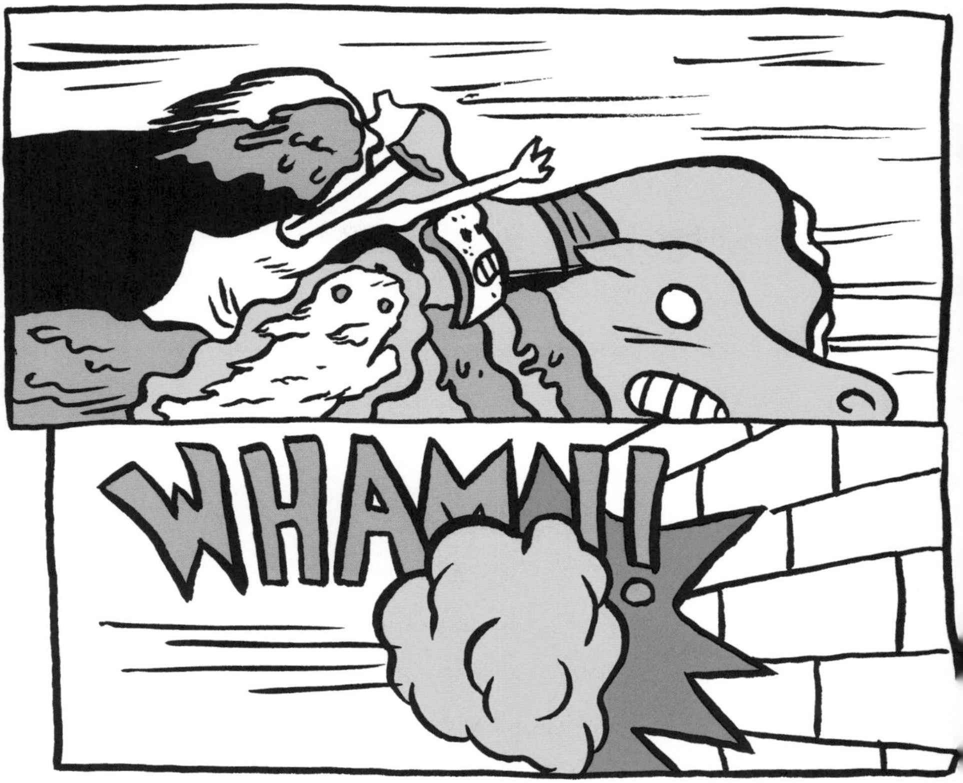
WHAM!!

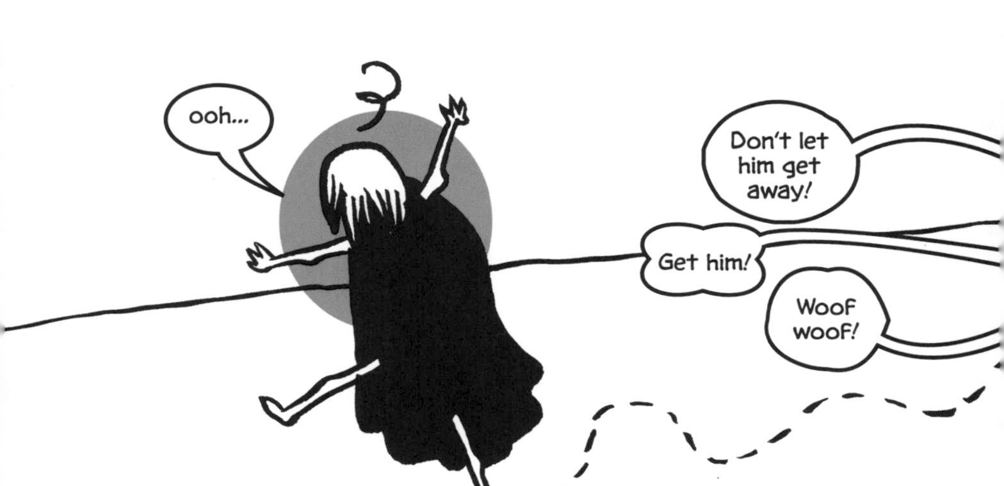
ooh...
Don't let him get away!
Get him!
Woof woof!

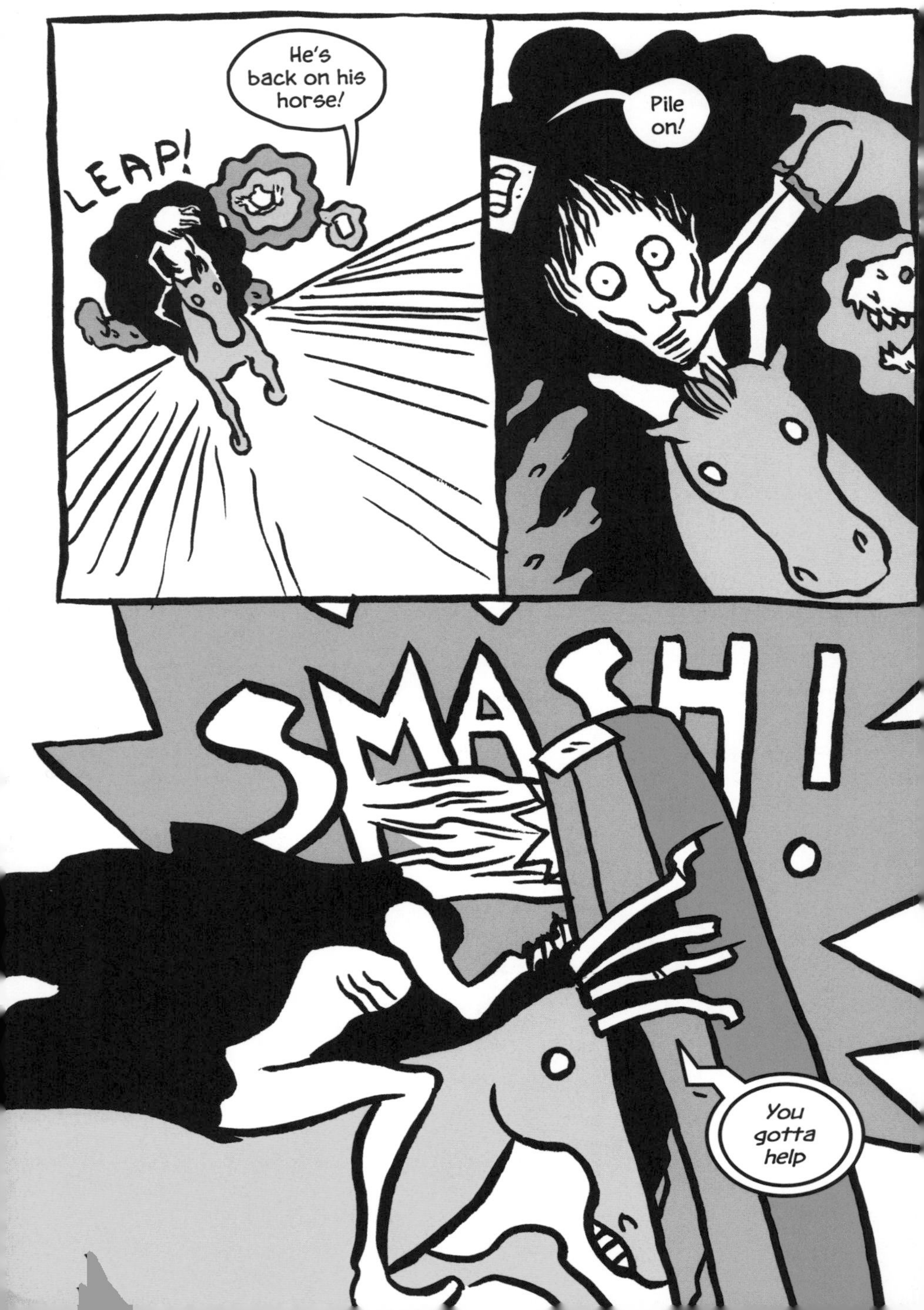
He's back on his horse!
LEAP!
Pile on!
SMASH!
You gotta help

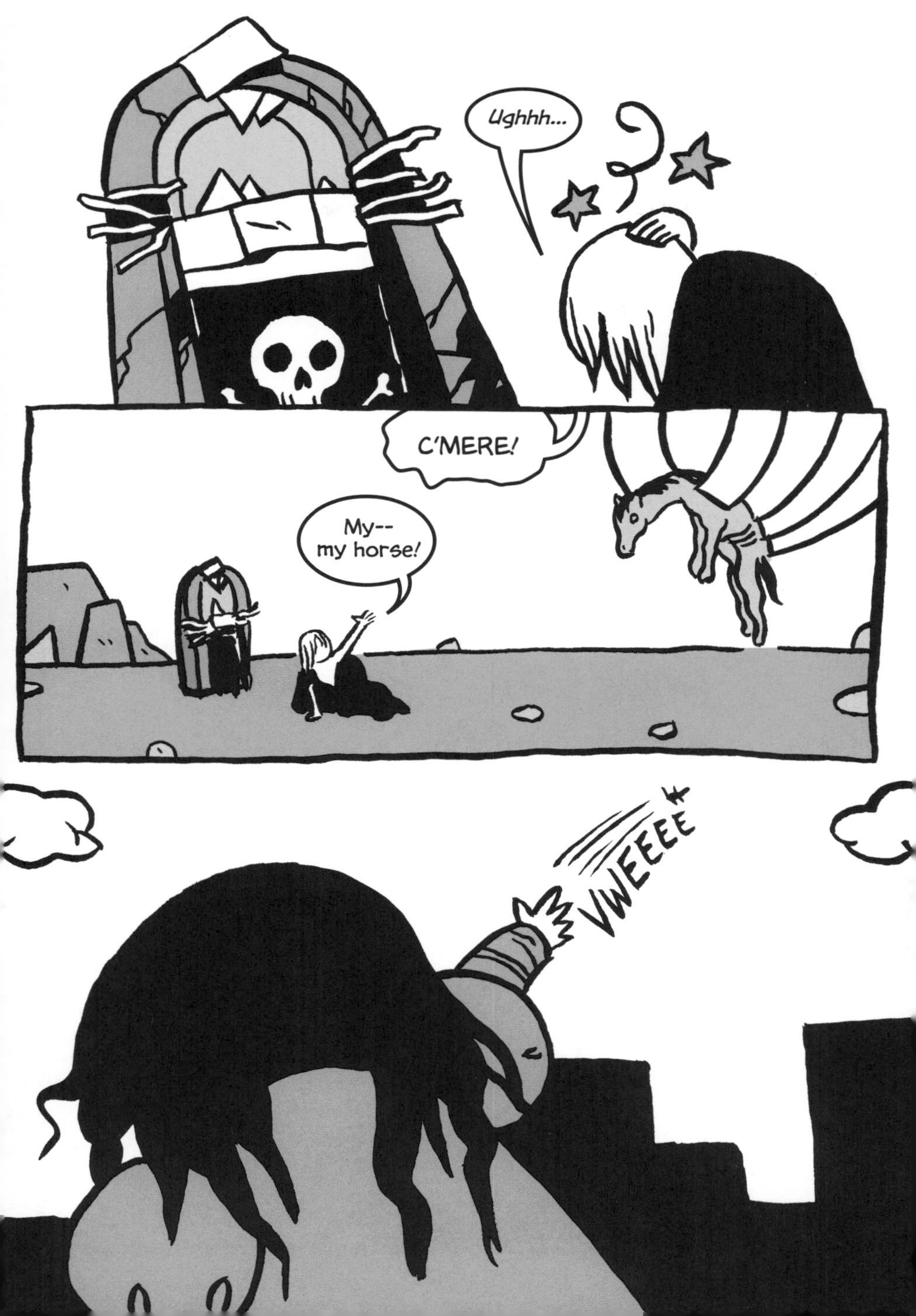
Ughhh...
C'MERE!
My-- my horse!
VWEEEE

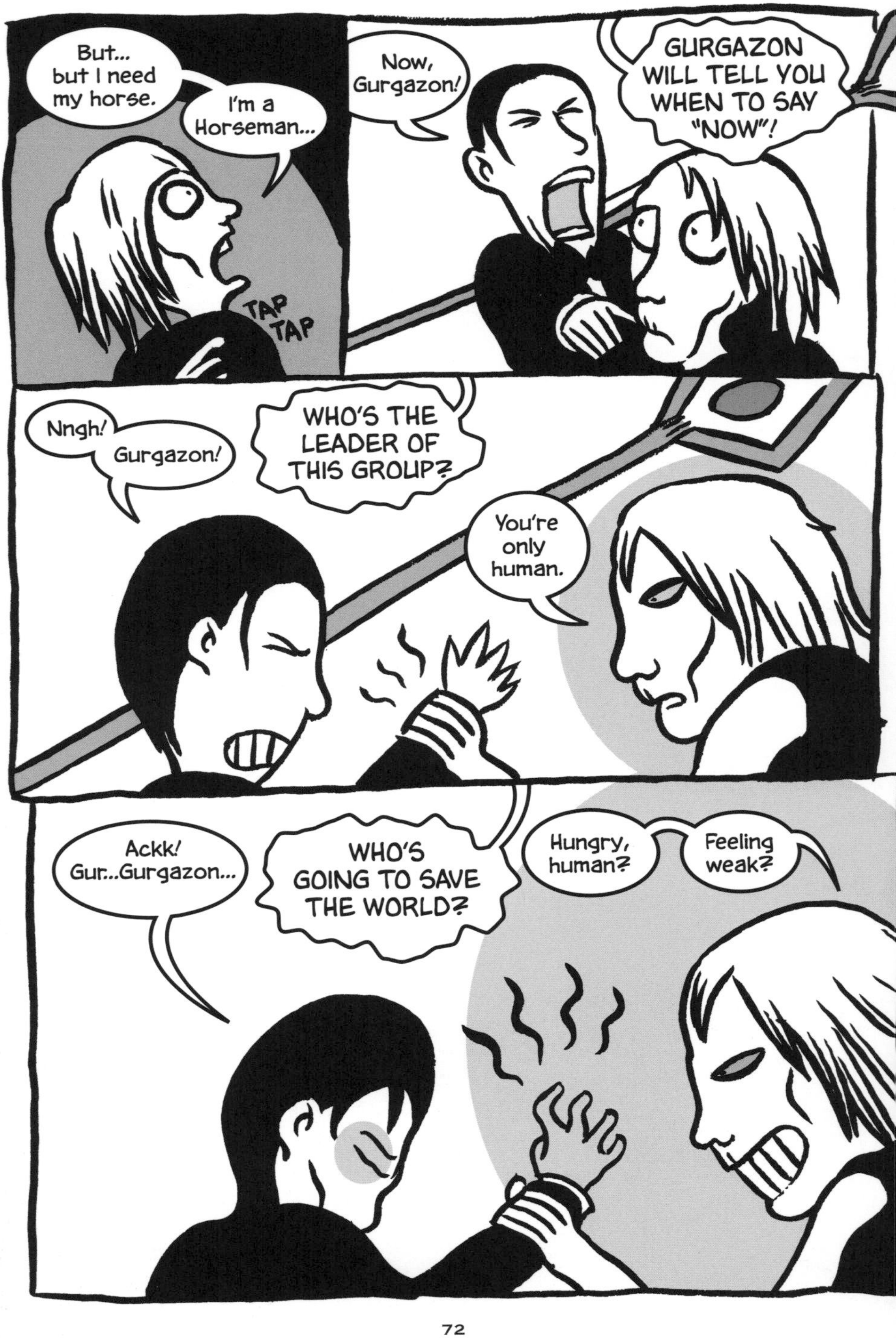
But...
but I need
my horse.
I'm a
Horseman...
TAP
TAP
Now,
Gurgazon!
GURGAZON
WILL TELL YOU
WHEN TO SAY
"NOW"!
Nngh!
Gurgazon!
WHO'S THE
LEADER OF
THIS GROUP?
You're
only
human.
Ackk!
Gur...Gurgazon...
WHO'S
GOING TO SAVE
THE WORLD?
Hungry,
human?
Feeling
weak?

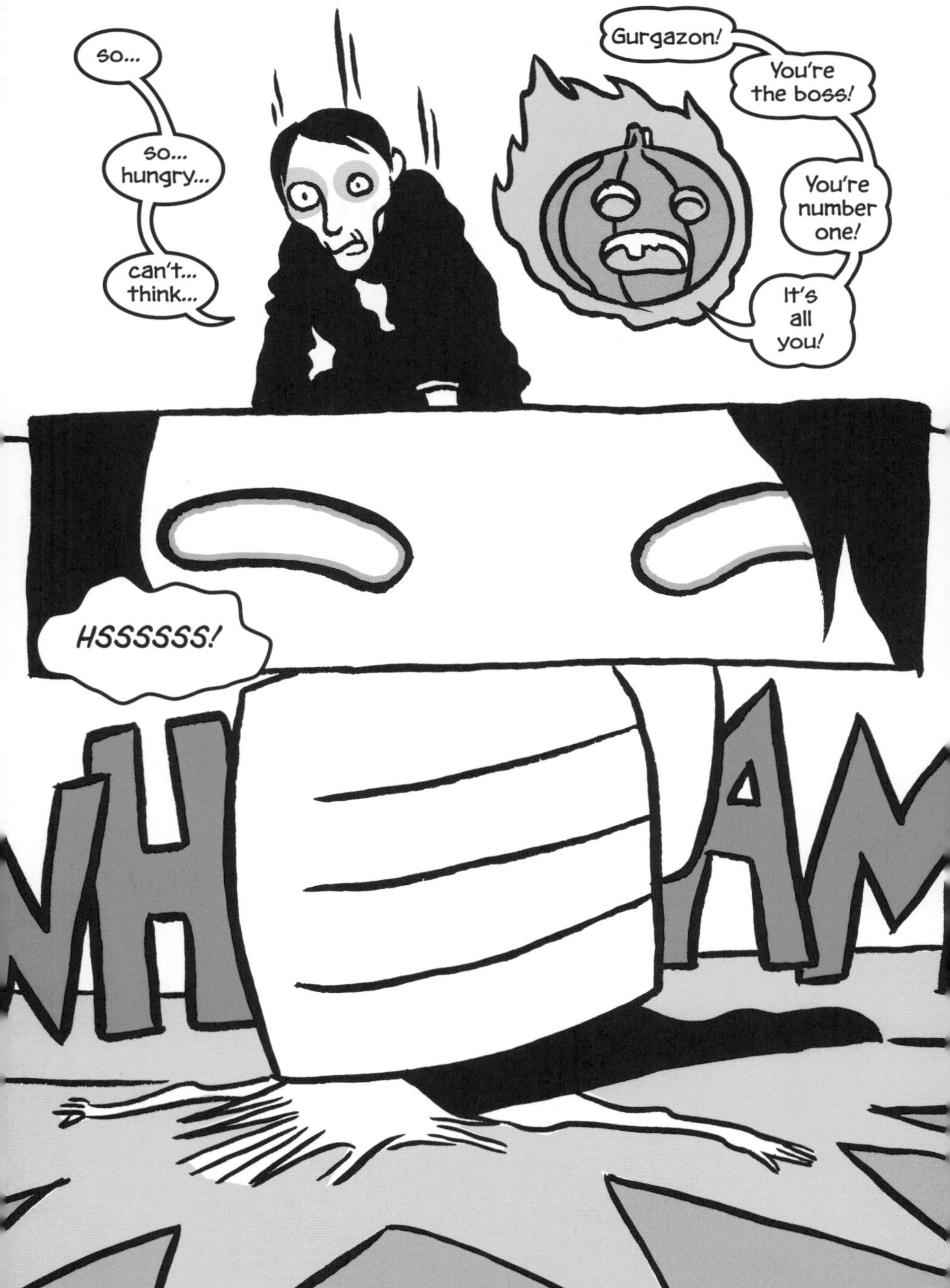
so...
so... hungry...
can't... think...
Gurgazon!
You're the boss!
You're number one!
It's all you!
HSSSSSS!
WHAM

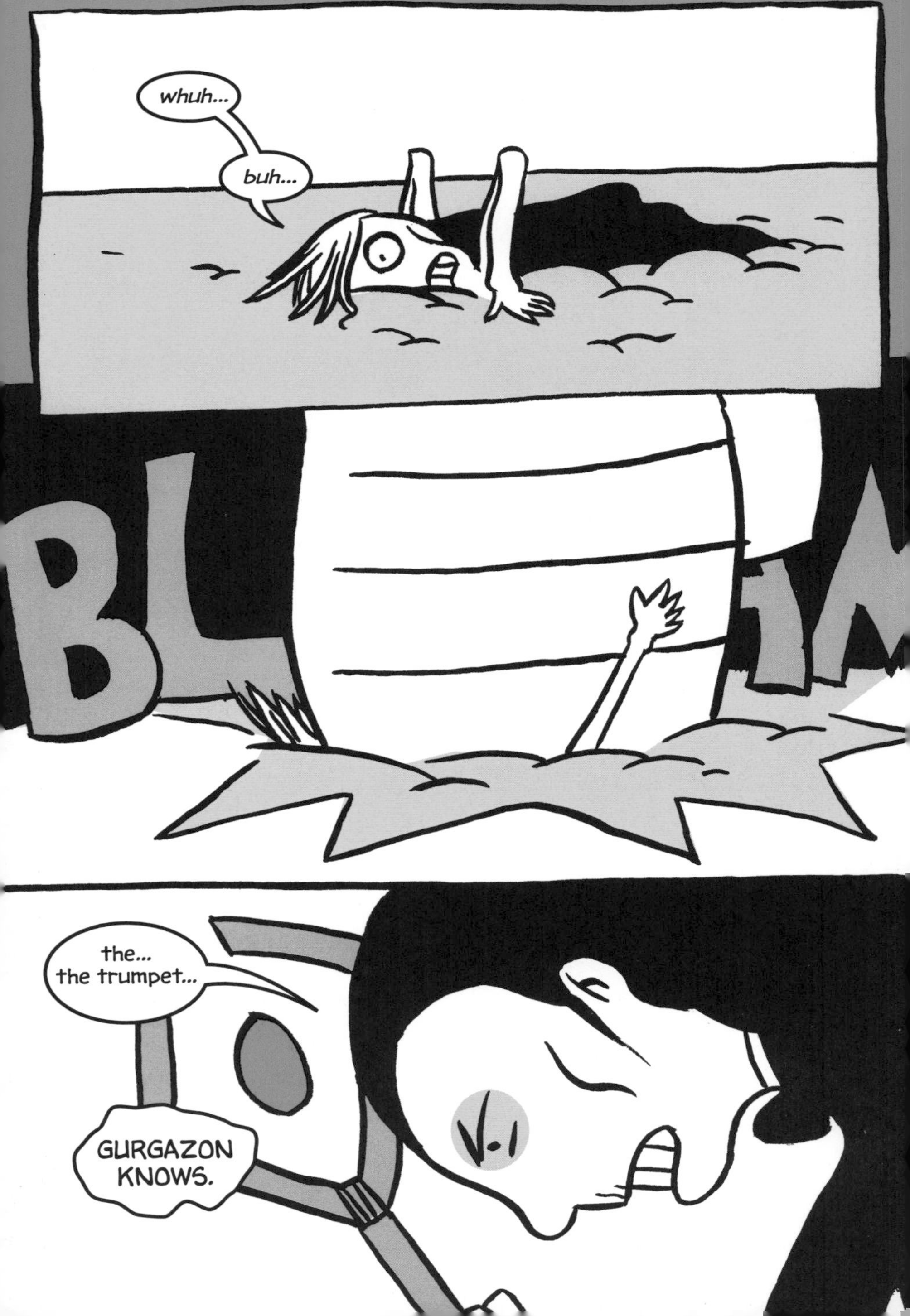
whuh...
buh...
BL
the...
the trumpet...
GURGAZON KNOWS.

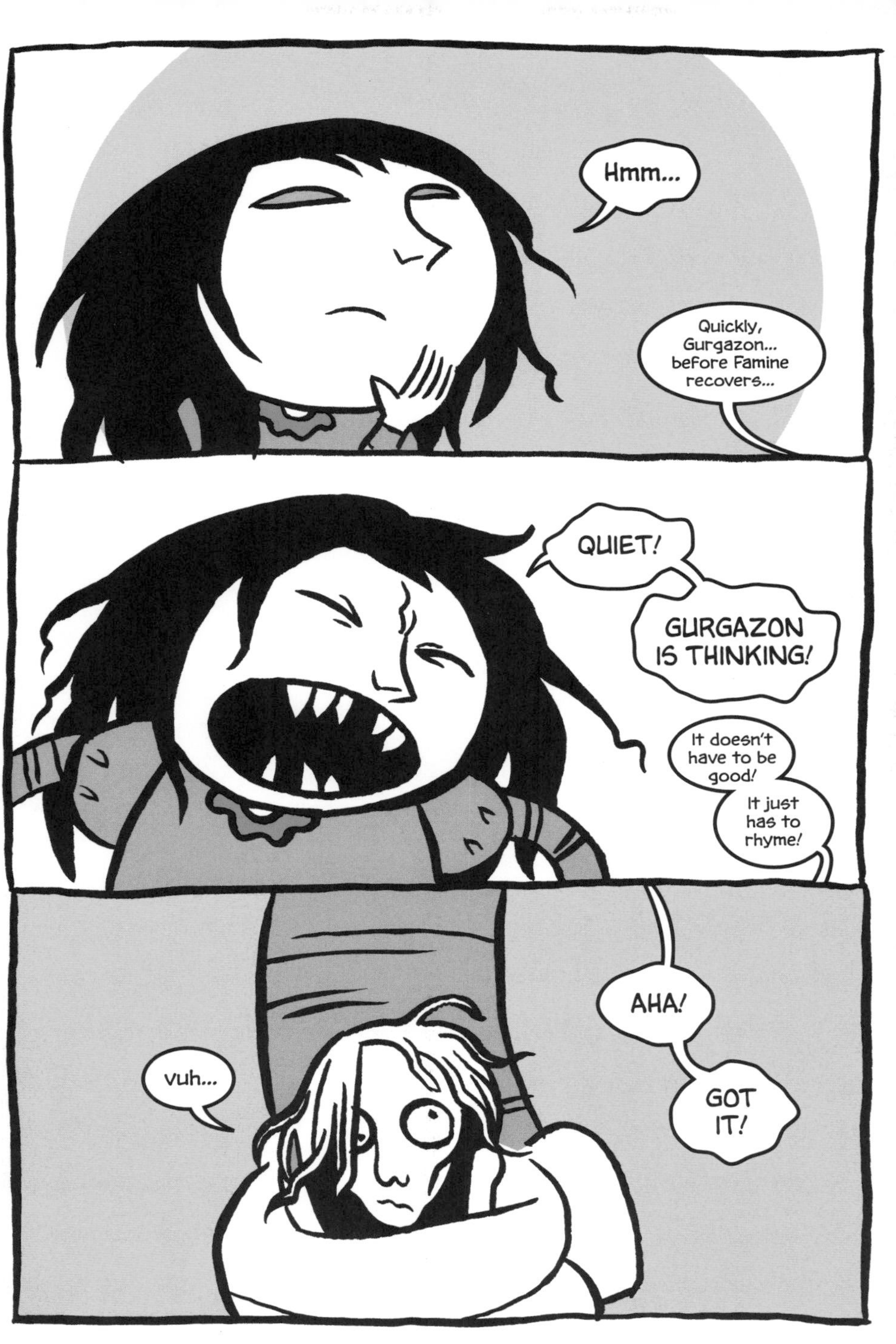
Hmm...
Quickly, Gurgazon... before Famine recovers...
QUIET!
GURGAZON IS THINKING!
It doesn't have to be good!
It just has to rhyme!
vuh...
AHA!
GOT IT!

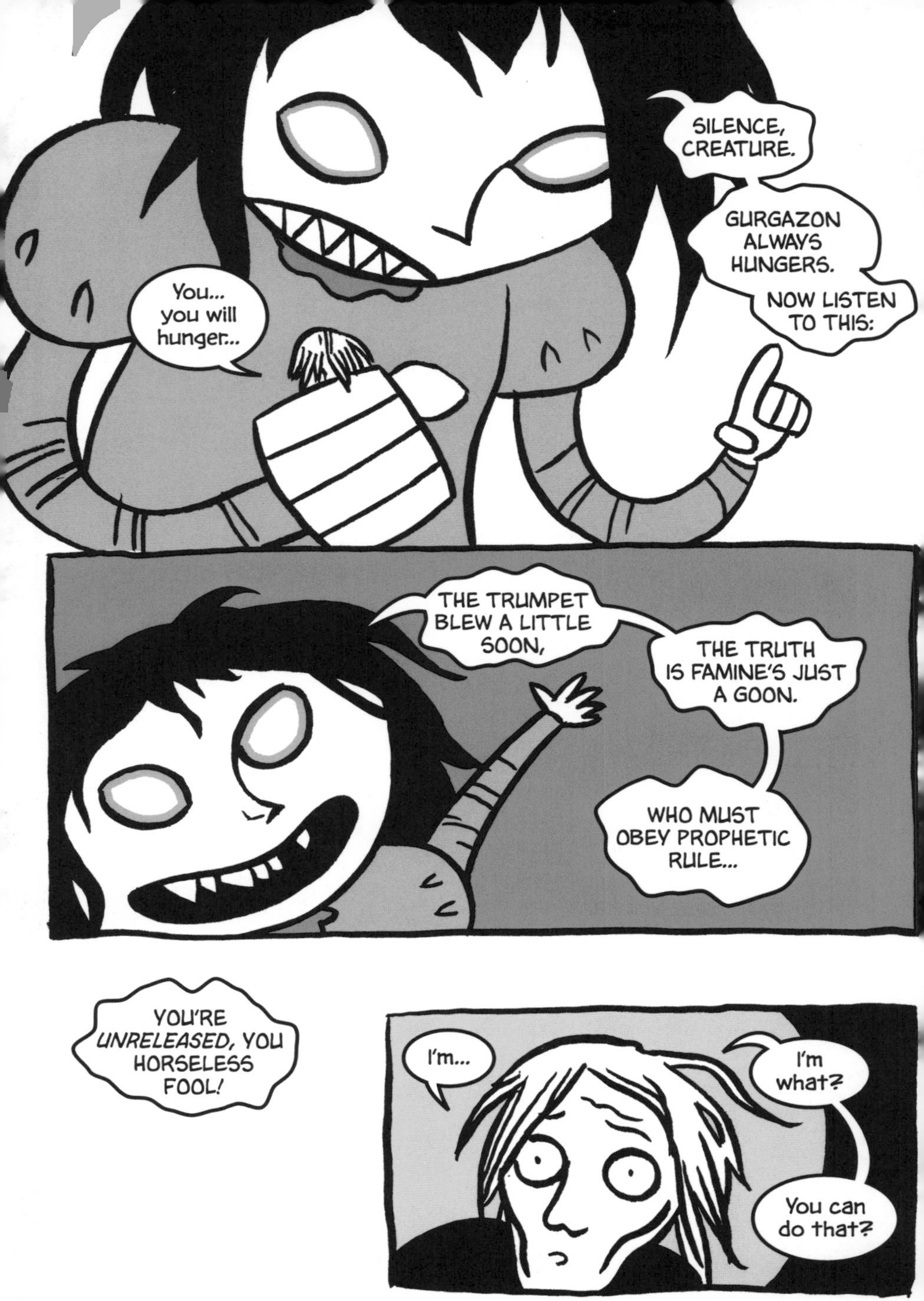
SILENCE, CREATURE.
GURGAZON ALWAYS HUNGERS.
NOW LISTEN TO THIS:
You... you will hunger...
THE TRUMPET BLEW A LITTLE SOON,
THE TRUTH IS FAMINE'S JUST A GOON.
WHO MUST OBEY PROPHETIC RULE...
YOU'RE *UNRELEASED*, YOU HORSELESS FOOL!
I'm...
I'm what?
You can do that?

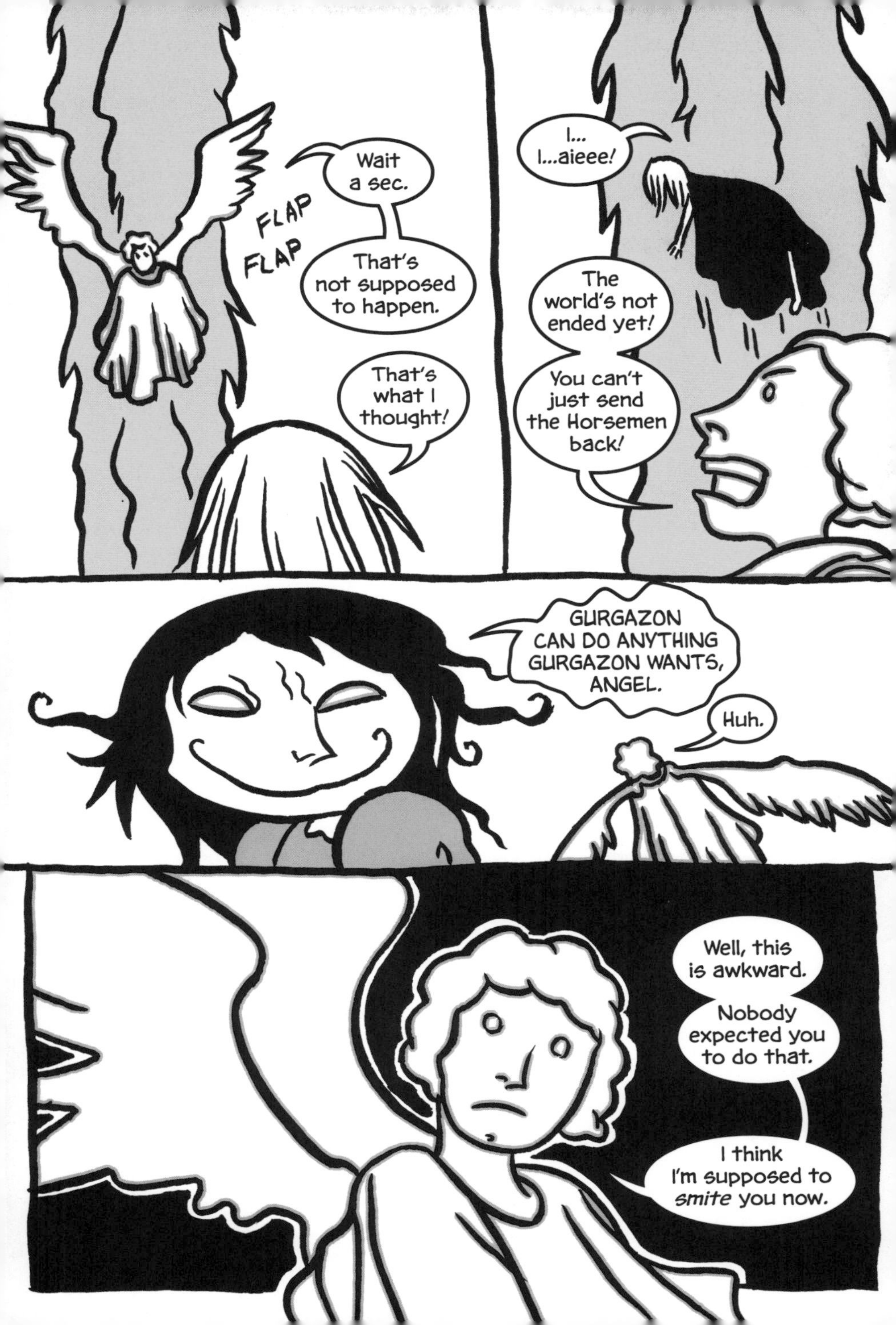

FLAP
FLAP
Wait a sec.
That's not supposed to happen.
That's what I thought!
I... I...aieee!
The world's not ended yet!
You can't just send the Horsemen back!
GURGAZON CAN DO ANYTHING GURGAZON WANTS, ANGEL.
Huh.
Well, this is awkward.
Nobody expected you to do that.
I think I'm supposed to *smite* you now.

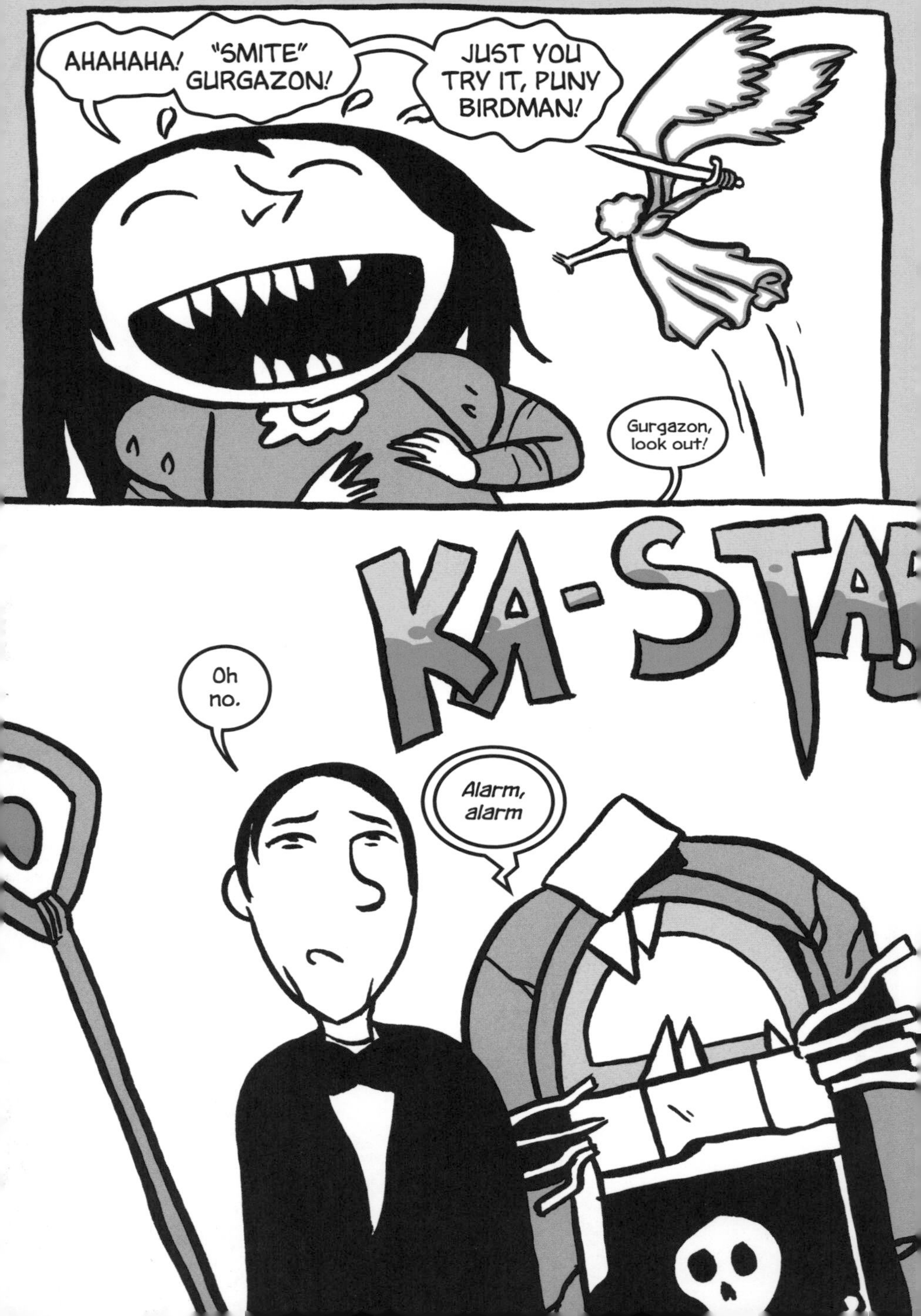
AHAHAHA!
"SMITE" GURGAZON!
JUST YOU TRY IT, PUNY BIRDMAN!
Gurgazon, look out!
KA-STA
Oh no.
Alarm, alarm

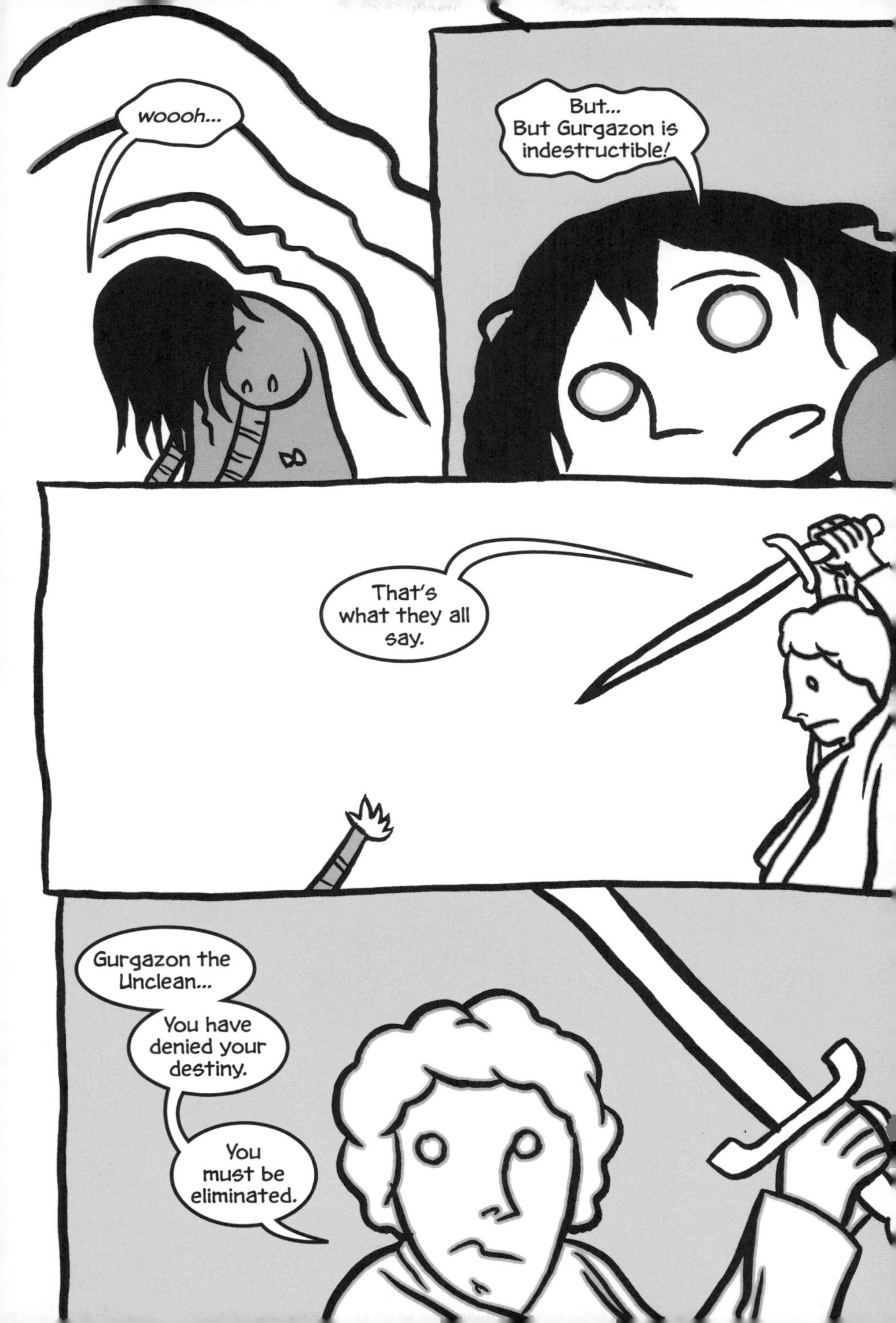
woooh...
But... But Gurgazon is indestructible!
That's what they all say.
Gurgazon the Unclean...
You have denied your destiny.
You must be eliminated.

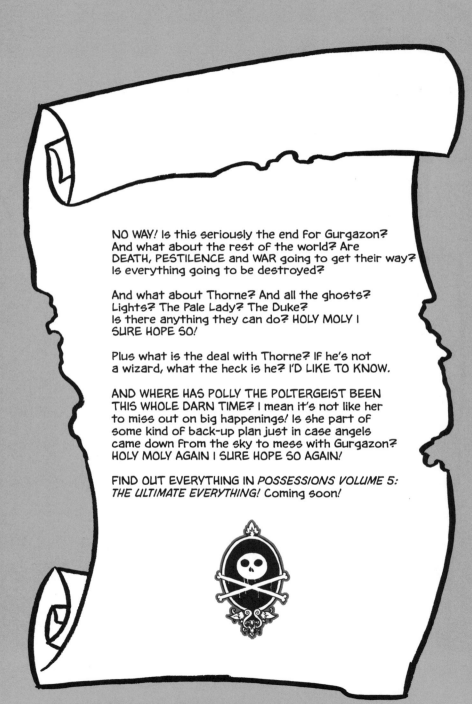

NO WAY! Is this seriously the end for Gurgazon?
And what about the rest of the world? Are
DEATH, PESTILENCE and WAR going to get their way?
Is everything going to be destroyed?

And what about Thorne? And all the ghosts?
Lights? The Pale Lady? The Duke?
Is there anything they can do? HOLY MOLY I
SURE HOPE SO!

Plus what is the deal with Thorne? If he's not
a wizard, what the heck is he? I'D LIKE TO KNOW.

AND WHERE HAS POLLY THE POLTERGEIST BEEN
THIS WHOLE DARN TIME? I mean it's not like her
to miss out on big happenings! Is she part of
some kind of back-up plan just in case angels
came down from the sky to mess with Gurgazon?
HOLY MOLY AGAIN I SURE HOPE SO AGAIN!

FIND OUT EVERYTHING IN *POSSESSIONS VOLUME 5:
THE ULTIMATE EVERYTHING!* Coming soon!

POSSESSIONS

BOOK FOUR

AUTHOR BIO

RAY FAWKES is a critically acclaimed writer and artist based in Toronto, Canada. His work has appeared online and in print around the world, and he is a two-time nominee for a Shuster award as "Outstanding Canadian Comic Book Writer." He ranges in style from dark, visceral horror (*Mnemovore*, *Black Strings*) to slapstick and black humor (*The Apocalipstix*), to literary and thought-provoking (*One Soul*, *The People Inside*), and has been published by DC/Vertigo, Oni Press, Tor.com, Top Shelf 2.0, White Wolf Publishing, and more.

www.rayfawkes.com

OTHER BOOKS FROM ONI PRESS

POSSESSIONS, BOOK ONE:
UNCLEAN GETAWAY
By Ray Fawkes
88 pages • Softcover
Black and white and sickly green interior
ISBN 978-1-934964-36-1

POSSESSIONS, BOOK TWO:
THE GHOST TABLE
By Ray Fawkes
88 pages • Softcover
Black and white and bone-chilling blue interior
ISBN 978-1-934964-61-3

POSSESSIONS, BOOK THREE:
THE BETTER HOUSE TRAP
By Ray Fawkes
88 pages • Softcover
Black and white and putrid pink interior
ISBN 978-1-934964-76-7

COURTNEY CRUMRIN
VOLUME 1: THE NIGHT THINGS
By Ted Naifeh
136 pages • Hardcover • Color interior
ISBN 978-1-934964-77-4

MERMIN, VOLUME 1:
OUT OF WATER
By Joey Weiser
152 pages • Hardcover • Color interior
ISBN 978-1-934964-98-9

SKETCH MONSTERS, VOLUME 1:
ESCAPE OF THE SCRIBBLES
By Joshua Williamson and Vicente Navarrete
48 pages • Hardcover • Color interior
ISBN 978-1-934964-69-9

BAD MACHINERY, VOLUME 1:
THE CASE OF THE TEAM SPIRIT
By John Allison
136 pages • Softcover • Color interior
ISBN 978-1-62010-084-4

For more information on these and other fine Oni Press comic books and graphic novels, visit www.onipress.com. To find a comic specialty store in your area, call 1-888-COMICBOOK or visit www.comicshops.us.

www.onipress.com